OF SNOW SO WHITE

FOREVER AFTER: CRIMSON SNOW
BOOK ONE

SIERRA ROWAN

MOUNTAIN TREE PRESS

Proofreading: Editing by Kimberly Dawn and Happy Ever Author

eBook ISBN: 978-1-955991-02-5
Paperback ISBN: 978-1-955991-13-1
Hardcover ISBN: 978-1-955991-21-6

First published in 2022
Urbana, IL, USA

v.0.4

AUTHOR'S NOTE

If you would like content guidance, please see the author's website at sierrarowan.com.

PROLOGUE
MELISANDRE

I'd never anticipated the moment of my victory would feel this sweet.

"You won't succeed."

I turned from the infant's cradle. Queen Eira's voice was weak, and an ever-expanding pool of her own red blood surrounded where she lay on the marble floor of her bedchambers. I'd considered tasting the delicious liquid, but moments like this couldn't be jeopardized for simple pleasures. Besides, I wanted no more trace of *her* in what I was about to do than existed already.

"I already have." I smiled at her from where I stood. Candlelight reflected from her blood and the glistening diamonds of her gown alike, making her shimmer like the snow for which she was named. "In a few moments, you'll be gone and everything you loved will be mine. I'd say that is quite the victory, wouldn't you?"

"The giants will stop you. They'll stop all of you."

"Oh, I'll deal with the giants."

Pain twisted her face, and her breaths came hard.

Lurches of her silk-clad chest made her entire body shake. I'd witnessed death a hundred times, caused it a hundred more, and I'd never found it as satisfying as this.

"You thought you could escape," I told her. "That you could save those old fools. That ruling Aneira as their queen would mean I couldn't claim the throne. But I told you when my sisters and I tore down your precious Jeweled Coven and bathed the stones of your sanctuary in the coven's blood that nothing would stand in our way, and all your efforts after the Witch War haven't changed a thing." I turned, looking down at the child. "You only gave us another tool for our future reign."

In her bassinet, the baby screwed up her face, her pale cheeks reddening as she began to cry. Silken strands of hair as dark as night lay on her head, a gift from her father, while her lips were like her mother's, bright as rubies.

But soon...

My fangs slid into place, and when I glanced back, Eira gasped. My lips curled. I enjoyed her fear.

Lifting my wrist, I slid my fangs lightly across my skin. Blood welled from the cuts.

Frantic words in the old tongue came from behind me, and my temper flared. With a sharp gesture, I cast a shattering spell and heard Eira's pained cry as her bones broke.

I smiled, returning my attention to the child. My blood dripped from my wrist, splashing on the baby's lips. The infant girl's face screwed up with confusion at the sudden rain of red liquid, but her mouth and throat moved, swallowing it down. "That's right, little one. That's right."

The baby whimpered, her confused expression turning to fear as the blood went to work.

"White as snow..."

I glanced back at the weak whisper. Her body broken, Eira lay with her gaze locked on the bassinet. Her chest barely moved with her faint breaths, and her skin had lost almost every trace of its color. The pool around her had stopped spreading, nearly all her life spilled out.

"Red as blood..."

I scoffed. "What is this? What are you doing?"

"Dark as ebony... I send the seven to my daughter..." Eira's gaze crept up to mine, burning with certainty. "And you will never win."

The light faded from her eyes.

My brow furrowing, I stared at her. That was no spell I'd ever heard. What foolishness had the dying witch queen attempted?

The baby began to cry again.

I turned back to the child. My blood was nearly gone from her little lips, swallowed away by an infant whose instinct was to drink down whatever was given to her. I chuckled. It was no matter. The queen was dead, and my plan was in motion. The twisted creatures of the empty realms would never claim me now.

Running my tongue along the tips of my fangs, I considered simply ending it now and freeing myself of the hold the Voidborn had upon me. But an infant wouldn't appease them. No, the forces my sisters and I had summoned that fateful night demanded a price for their gift, and though the Voidborn were willing to wait, the clock was ticking over us all.

But we'd found a loophole, each of us, and mine was screwing up her little face to cry again, perhaps sensing that her mother lay dead only a few feet away.

I let my fangs retract and willed myself to take the

appearance of a human once more. Picking up the infant, I cradled her to my chest. Beyond the heavy door of the queen's chambers, I could hear the sounds of footsteps. The king, perhaps, come to check on his wife, where instead he'd find the woman who would become his bride.

"Hush now, little one." I rocked the child. "I'm going to take good care of you."

1

GWYNEIRA

Nineteen years later

"—And then the Crown Prince of Gentresqua will arrive with his two brothers, and you'll say?"

Wincing at how the wooden back of my chair cut into my spine, I sighed. The fire at my side made the air of the study feel stifling, while the thin sunlight pouring through the tall windows was just bright enough to prevent any chance of a nap. "My, what big ears you have."

"Princess!" Harran pressed his free palm to the papers in his grip like a judge touching a book of law. "The prince of Gentresqua may well be a suitor for your hand soon. If your father should choose him or one of his brothers—"

"Father won't, not without asking me." My skin crawled, same as it did at the thought of any arranged marriage. Only a handful of prospects were left after the Witch War and the Giant War both erased so many nations from the map, but every suitor still out there filled me with dread.

Villagers and common folk liked to tell stories about love

being chosen by the gods. About lovers fated for each other, drawn together by destiny. I adored every romance story I could find, from the old tales to the dirty ones no one would have ever permitted me to read had they known I'd found them, and I surely spent far more time in the library than was ever considered proper for a young lady, but I'd never been able to make myself believe such a love would ever happen for me. Not when political realities were far more powerful than fairy tales.

But even though I had no idea who I'd end up forced to marry, I knew down to my bones they'd never be right for me. What *right* looked like, I couldn't successfully describe. But it wasn't some puffed-up royal, determined to treat me like nothing more than a brood mare for his heirs.

I gave Harran a flat look. "I am not interested in the tyrants of Gentresqua."

"Regardless, I shouldn't need to remind you of the need for civility. Now, what will you say to the prince?"

I rolled my eyes. "Nothing, Harran. I'll say nothing. Because Father needs to discuss the border situation with the envoy from Cioloren before we are going to be back on friendly enough terms to invite Gentresqua anywhere near the palace."

Harran blinked and looked down at his notes, alarm on his narrow face. "I... I don't have any details regarding—"

"She's right," my father called from the doorway of the grand hall, amusement in his voice. "Though how you managed to hear that when I only received word last night that Gentresqua has refused to visit until after Cioloren's envoy has a chance to speak with us, I am not sure."

I grinned, jumping up from my seat. "A little bird told me."

The skin around his blue eyes wrinkled as he smiled. "And where might I find this bird who spills state secrets?"

"In the north hall, three stones left of the door to the southern storage and just west of the stained-glass window that some artist thought looked like Aunt Gileska, though he surely needs his eyes checked."

Father laughed. "You found another spot where the sounds echo. What would I do without your careful examination of the castle?"

"What else am I supposed to do when Stepmother won't let me leave?"

His smile faded. "She only worries for you, Gwyneira. As do I."

"There's no *reason*. The Witch War ended before I was even born. The Giant War was over a decade ago. You have most of the giants in prison, and the Warden Wall will keep the rest out of the capital. Erenelle itself is a wasteland locked behind magical barriers that even its own people can't get through. The giants are not a threat to—"

"That's what we believed when you were a baby."

I scowled, looking away.

"We have the giants, yes, but none of them have confirmed who was responsible for your mother's death. And until we can be sure, we can't risk that any Erenlian who escaped us might not try again, even with the Wall."

"No one has disappeared in *years*, Father."

"Whole nations are still gone. The Wild Lands continue to be overrun by chaotic magic, and we lost the last three expeditions that tried to locate the kingdom of Zenirya." He sighed, putting a hand to my shoulder in that way he had, trying to comfort me even if physical displays of affection never came naturally to him. "I know it grates at you. It grates at me too. But the security of our nation and our future depends upon caution. Your stepmother knows this. It's why she's sworn to protect you always, just as she did the night your mother died."

I sighed, tired of the old argument. The gods knew I remembered the story. I'd only heard it a thousand times. Old friends from before her time as queen, my mother had invited Melisandre to stay with us at the castle. But one night, giants angry that my father would not cede his claim to our ancestral lands had scaled the walls and attacked, seeking to strike Father where it would hurt the most. Working together, Melisandre and my mother fought them, but even they were barely a match for the Erenlians, whose inborn command of magic rendered them overwhelmingly powerful. My mother fell, her body crushed by their brute strength, but with her dying breath, she'd cast a spell, propelling them through the ether back to where they'd come from.

My father had come then to find his wife dead and a terrified Melisandre cradling me while I cried. In the years since, Melisandre had guarded me at every turn, crafting the magical Warden Wall to keep the giants out, sending away anyone who she suspected of siding with them, and insisting I stay inside as much as possible, lest assassins see me. Even time in the gardens was limited, and going beyond the castle into the capital city of Lumilia?

Unthinkable.

Sometimes, I wondered if Melisandre's wounds from that night had only healed on the outside, leaving those on the inside to fester and become a paranoia that saw enemies around every turn.

She only ever said that protecting me was the least she could do for my poor, fallen mother.

"So what are we to do if Gentresqua doesn't agree to end the border dispute?" I asked, changing the subject.

My father sighed. "Envoys from Cioloren have agreed to speak to them. The Gentresquans are being stubborn, since the giants were significant contributors to their economy. They can't see the danger those creatures presented. But they'll come around." He shook his head. "We *must* have unity. For all our sakes."

He pushed the frustration from his face. "But enough of that. Are you ready for the party this evening?"

I gave him a wry look. "I can be more help to you than just as a decoration at a party, Father."

"You and I both know you're more than a *decoration*, Gwyneira, so listen well tonight. Glean any information you can." The corner of his mouth rose. "See if you can't give Harran a few more moments of panic."

I laughed. Standing nearby, the old steward frowned, his hands still clutching his notes. "Yes, your highness," I told my father.

He grinned. Patting my shoulder one last time, he gave the steward a nod and then walked away.

I glanced at Harran. "Are we done? I should really get ready."

Irritation crossed the steward's face, but with a futile look at his notes, he gestured with one hand for me to go. "Yes, Princess."

I headed for the corridor as well, hooking a left and hurrying along the sloping hall as it curved up toward the higher levels. Servants moved out of my way swiftly, some of them chuckling at me. "Always running," one of them called.

I grinned. At the second highest floor, I started to turn and then caught sight of the highest level where my step-mother and father had their two chambers.

A flash of silver light flared against the stone wall just for a moment.

Curiosity made me pause. That hadn't looked like candlelight.

Was Melisandre doing one of her spells?

I hesitated, excitement and caution tangling in me. I'd never seen her do magic. She said it would be dangerous for me to see since I hadn't inherited any of that power from my mother. Father and I were magicless; witnessing her spell-craft could harm us.

Nevertheless, Melisandre still devoted herself to protecting us with her skills. But no matter how practicality tugged at me—the last thing I wanted was to go insane as she threatened, after all—I couldn't shake the desire to see her at work.

A murmur of angry voices bounced from the wall and I paused. Another echoing spot. The castle was full of them, not that anyone else seemed to notice. Servants and guards swore they never heard the things I did, but I could recount word for word all the conversations I was inadvertently privy to, courtesy of the way sound carried here. The halls were covered in tapestries dampening the places I'd found that echoed.

I glanced around and then moved half a step to the left.

"—not much longer. Have patience!"

A grunt of pain followed, and alarm shot through me. That was Stepmother's voice.

I ran up the sloping corridor. A short turn of the hall brought me to her door, which was cracked open just an inch.

She was on her knees before her large silver mirror, one hand to her throat and another bracing her on the thick fur rugs. Strands of her golden hair had fallen from their tight coif atop her head to hang in ringlets around her face. The curtains of her room were drawn, as always, but the candle-light cast her face in harsh relief, making the lines of her cheeks and jaw look sharper than I'd ever seen them. Her body shook, and she looked so pale it was frightening.

Something moved in the mirror.

My breath caught. Like fish in the garden pond, dark shapes slipped in and out of view beyond the silver surface. I couldn't tell what they were, but terror gripped me at the sight of them. Impressions of tentacles, of teeth and claws played through my mind, though I could never see the full shape of them. All around the gilded frame, shadows seemed to cling thicker and thicker to the carvings of apples and roses amid the metalwork vines, like encroaching night. Whispers swirled around me, just on the edge of hearing, crooning sibilant enticements for me to come closer, closer still, touch the mirror, just reach out and—

I took a step back. Oh, gods, one of her spells must have gone wrong.

Stepmother's head snapped up, her ice-blue eyes pinning me through the gap in the door. Rage flashed across her face.

I froze, new fear hitting me, unexpected and confusing. Gods help me, I'd never seen that expression from her before. She wasn't ever really *warm*, but she loved me. I knew that.

Shoving up from the rugs, she strode toward the door and the furious look vanished as if it had never been, washed away by the caring smile I knew so well. "Gwyneira, darling. What are you doing here?"

I stepped back as she opened the door and slipped outside. From her room, a strange murmur rose, only to be silenced when she shut the door firmly at her back, her compassionate smile never fading.

"I heard…" I glanced at the door briefly. "I thought you were in trouble."

She gave a small laugh and took my arm, leading me away from the room. "You're too sweet, my dear. I merely tripped on the rug."

"Oh." That didn't make sense. "But what were those—"

"What were what, dear?"

"In the mirror. I-I thought I saw—"

She laughed again, cutting off my words. "I didn't see anything, darling. It must have been a reflection of the candlelight."

I hesitated. "But—"

"It's a very old mirror, Gwyneira. The surface is warped and distorted with age. I only keep it around because it reminds me of dear friends I once knew. But it's quite useless for a good reflection, and the gods know it does odd things with candlelight."

I nodded slowly.

"Tell me," Stepmother said, her tone clearly changing the subject. "Are you ready for the party? I hear those delectable princes of Gentresqua will be there."

"Um, actually, they—"

"That's wonderful. Hurry and get dressed, yes? Sundown is coming soon."

I paused as we reached the opening to the spiraling corridor. "Are you sure you're okay?"

"Of course, darling. Now go on."

I started down the slope, casting a brief look back to see her still watching me with a smile. Returning the expression, I continued on, but curiosity gnawed at me. Candlelight had never made me think I saw monsters in the mirror before, let alone hear strange whispers or feel compulsions like I had.

But then, if she had been doing magic...

My steps sped up, carrying me away from the room faster. I definitely didn't want to go mad.

And maybe she'd just been angry that she'd tripped. Gods knew I wanted to kick the dresser every time I bumped into it by accident. And maybe the candlelight had made the mirror's surface seem odd.

As I reached my own floor of the castle, a shiver crept over my skin and I turned, looking back up the curving hall toward the upper level. Maybe it really was nothing.

But I couldn't shake the feeling something had been watching me.

2

MELISANDRE

That damn girl.

I stalked back to my chambers, glaring at the walls as I went. This accursed castle never stopped whispering to her, carrying sounds it had no right to carry and echoing them to her as if for her ears alone. I'd also locked that thrice-damned door, yet still it opened for her.

And it was getting worse.

The castle hated me, that much I knew. Stained by the blood of its dead queen, the building Eira had made her home resented my presence and did everything it could to sabotage me.

I shut my door behind me, quickly muttering a curse upon the lock before turning back to the room. "You won't change this. No matter what little tricks you play."

A quiver moved through the stones beneath me and I snarled. If I could, I'd burn this place to the ground. I hadn't had a decent sleep in nearly two decades, thanks to its little shifts and quivers whenever I tried to rest.

Spitting another curse at the room for good measure, I

looked back at the mirror. The creatures of the empty realms had seen her now. For nineteen years, I'd managed to keep that girl and her irritating father out of here, feeding those two idiots endless stories about magic being a danger to the uninitiated. Her father had been hard to convince—his late wife had been a witch, after all—but I made sure he came around. Meanwhile, Gwyneira adored me, trusting her "loving" stepmother like the naïve fool she was. She would have stayed away from my spellwork until she died of old age if left to her own devices.

And now the castle had seen fit to mess that up too.

Little did the damned building know it had just condemned its precious princess.

A twist of breeze signaled the arrival of one of my many servants, turned over the years and living in the shadowed depths of the castle. Few humans ever spotted them, and any who did only thought them ghosts.

After all, everyone knew they'd died.

"Should we follow the princess, Mistressss?" the man hissed around his fangs.

"Yes. Do not get too close."

From the corner of my eye, I saw him bow, his dead-pale skin snowy white in the shadows. He'd been a tailor, I thought. Maybe a stablehand.

It hardly mattered.

At the dismissive motion of my hand, he shifted form, becoming nothing more than a twist of darkness. The windows opened and then closed with his departure.

On legs I refused to let shake, I paced toward the mirror. The creatures beyond that magic surface moved like angry eels, flashing in and out of view. Had she seen them when she peered past that crack in the door? They'd seen *her*, I knew that. The Voidborn had called for her blood and soul in an instant, nearly pressing through into this world if only to reach her faster.

They wouldn't be delayed much longer.

A flash of hungry magic whipped out at me as I came near and I retreated, staying just beyond the reach of its ravenous tentacle. Mostly invisible to the untrained eye, the creatures beyond the mirror would appear as nothing but a shift of shadow.

The girl seemed like she'd seen more.

My fists clenched. She would never be a witch, not between the horror stories I'd told her and my blood inside her veins to boot. But her magical heritage made her the perfect substitute that no other man, woman, or child I turned could ever be.

They were only human, after all.

But she was Eira's daughter, and she had spent her life with my blood twisting her, deep down inside. The combination would make her the perfect sacrifice to satisfy my deal with these creatures once they finally feasted upon her.

I had only to kill her first.

The murmurs beyond the mirror grew louder. They wouldn't be patient much longer. I'd hoped to wait until she was married to one of those damn princes, her whole life of love and family and ruling a kingdom ahead of her—a well of untapped potential to satiate the bloodthirsty Voidborn for centuries—before I finally fulfilled the plan I'd put in place years ago.

But now would have to do.

I crossed to the vanity, taking up a small vial amid the dozen I kept there. Most were perfume. A few were spells. But this one...

A flick of shadow left the mirror, wrapping around and then passing briefly through the red glass vial.

My lips curled. The beings of the empty realms approved, as well they should.

Nineteen years of waiting ended tonight.

3
GWYNEIRA

Corsets were invented by the devil.

A gasp left me as Fironia tugged the criss-crossed ribbons tighter on my back. "Do we"—I grunted against the pressure on my ribs—"really need it this... ow... tight?"

"The queen has ordered it, my lady."

I cast a look over my shoulder. "What?"

My maid's heart-shaped face reddened. "She says you slouch, my lady."

"I do not!"

Fironia wouldn't meet my eyes as she set to tying the laces.

"I need to *breathe*," I insisted. A heartbeat passed. "Please, Fironia. *If* I even slouch in the first place, I promise I won't tonight for your sake, okay? She'll never know you didn't tighten them all the way."

The maid's dark eyes flicked up to me briefly, and then she started loosening the ties.

A rush of air entered my lungs. "Thank you."

I caught a flash of her smile before she ducked her face away.

Taking a few more breaths with relief, I returned my attention to the mirror. My gown for the party hung on the wardrobe behind me, a confection of layers upon layers of pale lace and red silk. By any estimation, it was stunning.

"All done, my lady." Fironia turned, retrieving the dress from its hanger. "If you please?"

I nodded and turned for her to assist me.

"You look beautiful, Princess," Fironia said when she was finished lacing and buttoning me into the luxurious dress.

I bit my lip. The dress fell around me like waves of a frothing blood-red sea. Around my midsection, it cinched in before rising to my chest, leaving the tops of my breasts and my neck exposed. A trim of lace that glistened like snowfall circled that edge and continued over my shoulders and around my back.

"Here, my lady. Your stepmother sent these for you as well."

I glanced away from the mirror. Fironia held a tiny red vial and a pendant in her hands.

"This is in case you wish to use it tonight." She handed me the small vial, and I tucked it into the waistband of the dress. "A touch of perfume, she said. And this she had specially crafted for you."

Fironia fastened the chain around my neck. An apple pendant that looked carved from a single ruby reflected the light back so beautifully, I'd swear the shadows in my room recoiled from its glistening red glow.

I brushed my fingertips over the gem and then paused. "Why is it so cold?"

"I do not know, my lady. Perhaps it was stored some-where cool?"

I nodded, unable to take my eyes from the apple in the mirror. The light caught on its surface and yet seemed to glimmer from within as well, a testimony to the exquisite craftsmanship of the artisan who'd carved it. Neither too large nor too small, it hung at the base of my throat like it had been measured precisely to fit there.

"It's beautiful," I said. "I'll be sure to thank—"

A scream came from the hall.

For a heartbeat, the sound froze me, and then I turned, grabbing up my dress and running for the door as quickly as I could. Footsteps pounded on the stone floor, and when Fironia yanked open the door, I saw the guards racing by.

Heading for the upper floor.

"What's going on?" I cried, but none of them answered. Clutching my skirts, I ran after them as quickly as I could. A crowd had already begun to gather on the top level, surrounding the hallway to my father's chambers.

Panic drummed a fast beat in my chest. "What's happened?" I demanded.

"My lady." Harran pushed through the crowd, his aged face a picture of worry. "Perhaps you shouldn't—"

I shoved past him.

Guards blocked the door to my father's chamber, tension in every line of their bearing.

"Move!" I ordered them.

They stayed still, their eyes flicking toward me and then away.

"Princess, please," Harran called from behind me. "You shouldn't—"

"Let her in."

My stepmother's voice carried from beyond the door. With a flash of reluctance on their faces, the guards stepped aside while one of them opened the door fully.

Horror stole my breath. "Father!"

I pushed past the guards and ran to him, crashing to my knees beside where he lay on the bearskin rug. His skin was gray. His eyes stared at the ceiling, unblinking.

"Father, no. Please!" I fumbled at his neck, feeling for his pulse.

Nothing.

"No, please." I pressed a hand to his cheek, but his sightless eyes never wavered from their empty stare into the beyond. "Please!"

A sob caught in my throat, on the verge of becoming a scream. This wasn't real. This couldn't be happening.

Oh, by the gods, somebody let me wake up.

Hands took my shoulders, pulling me away. I threw a look back to find the guardsmen holding me. "Wh-what happened?" I cried as they hauled me to my feet.

"Poison." My stepmother's voice was thick with grief. With a quick motion, she gestured to someone behind me. "You. Maid girl."

Blinking nervously, Fironia slipped past the guards, giving me a worried look as she passed. "Y-yes, your highness?"

Melisandre waved a hand for her to come closer and then whispered something in her ear.

Fironia's face went still. "Yes, my lady."

Her voice was distant, and when she straightened again, she was as expressionless as a stone. She seemed to be staring at nothing, her eyes locked on some middle distance above my father's body.

"Guards." My stepmother pushed to her feet. "Search the princess."

I gasped as their hands moved over my skirts, roughly patting me down. One of them drew out the red vial of perfume.

"You treacherous child." Melisandre strode past my father's body. "How could you?"

"What? I—"

She struck me hard across the face, sending me reeling as pain erupted in my cheek.

"This was found beside the king." My stepmother held up a vial identical to the one the guards had taken. "And now another is in her possession. Tell me, stepdaughter, were you planning to poison me too? Was waiting for the throne until we died of old age not good enough for you?"

"What? That's not mine! You gave that to me!"

Melisandre scoffed. "Maid?"

"It is hers, my lady. I have seen it in her room many times."

I stared at Fironia, horrified. Her words were distant, and her face was as blank as a doll's. She wouldn't even look at me.

"She's lying!" I shouted. "I would never—"

"Silence!"

I gasped, my throat constricting like a lump had lodged squarely inside it, as if I'd swallowed something and it was choking me. Against my skin, the apple pendant burned with cold and my hand flew to it, but I couldn't pull it away from my neck.

"Guards, take her to the dungeon. I shall be down to deal with her shortly, once we have shown her father the respect he *should* have been afforded by his only child."

The soldiers yanked me around. Harran and the other servants stared at me in horror, but they backed away to make room as the guards hauled me toward the door.

My mouth moved, the burning pendant on my throat trapping my cries of innocence as the guards dragged me away.

4

DEX

"You're not going to like this."

Blinking my tired eyes in the candlelight, I looked up from the map of the latest caverns we'd excavated. We'd only gotten home an hour ago from yet another day in the mines, and I needed to finish this evaluation of the area we'd uncovered before I could call it a night.

Assuming Clay hadn't shrunk our beds again. All these years and that man still didn't think that joke had gotten old. "What now?"

Byron leaned back from the magic mirror on his desk. "Activity in Aneira."

I lifted an eyebrow at the copper-haired scholar.

"Soldiers lining the castle walls," he elaborated. "Looks like something big happened."

I didn't ask for more, setting the maps aside and then pushing to my feet out of my leather armchair. Crossing to Byron's desk, I bent down to get a better angle on the mirror as the man moved aside.

It took a moment for the image to focus. Magic mirrors were temperamental, and this one obeyed Byron more than anyone else. But after a few seconds, it decided to trust me.

My jaw clenched at the sight of the Aneiran capital of Lumilia. The stone roads were lined by white-walled buildings, each structure trimmed in dark wood and decorated with windows of multicolored glass. Steep rooftops stood ready to sluff off snow and rain, and brass lantern posts dotted every street to provide illumination at night. At its heart, the castle rose in stark gray stone, a fortress dotted with towers and surrounded by a crenelated wall with a massive gate, all of it hiding countless secrets within. It'd been nearly twenty years since I'd stood at that gate, and the damn place hadn't changed a bit.

Though the gods knew I had.

I concentrated on what mattered, not decades-old memories. Byron hadn't been wrong, those Aneirans were worked up over something. Soldiers were running along the pathways atop the crenelated wall, their commanders barking orders behind them. To a person, they held weapons, and when they stopped at their designated stations, they gripped their spears and swords like they were expecting the sky itself to rain fire upon them. On the castle walls at their backs, black cloths fluttered down, draping over the flags that hung from the windows.

My gut dropped. "Oh, fuck."

"What?"

"Someone's dead. Royal."

Silence greeted my words.

I leaned away from the mirror. Byron's face had gone bloodless beneath the scattering of freckles on his cheeks.

"*That* many soldiers..." He shook his head. "They're not simply preparing in case someone takes advantage of the change in leadership."

"Assassin, probably."

"Gods..." He turned away, raking his hands through his copper curls as he swore rapidly in the old tongue of the giants and several other languages besides. I didn't speak a damn one of them—he'd been trained as a scholastic monk in the Order of Berinlian; I'd trained in the school of "try not to get killed on the battlefield"—but I understood the sentiment.

Not to mention the burgeoning panic behind it.

Drawing a slow breath, I looked back at the mirror as I fought the wave of adrenaline rising in me over all my memories of the *last* time an Aneiran royal died. Nearly twenty years ago, I'd barely been more than a grunt in the Aneiran army, passing as human and happy to defend the nation I'd called home ever since the giants drove me out of Erenelle as a young child. Hell, I'd even believed it when the Aneiran king said the Erenlians murdered his wife. Giants would've killed me just for being born "different" from them, after all. They would've killed all seven of us who now called this cabin home, and we'd each only survived through luck. Was it such a stretch to believe they'd murder someone else, no matter how peaceful they claimed to be?

Except the giants hadn't been prepared for the backlash. Hadn't even seemed to know it was coming. Those first few towns we attacked on the border of Erenelle barely possessed a military, and the rest had fought us with weapons so old, they likely predated the village elders.

And I'd started to wonder if my superiors were wrong.

But the king and his new bride in the Aneiran capital

hadn't given a damn. Not when countless giants died. Not when the leaders in the nation of Erenelle rushed to mount a defense. Not when the war grew bloody on both sides.

To this day, I woke from nightmares of the horrors I'd seen.

"Any sign of the witch queen?" Byron asked.

I scanned the walls and then shook my head. "Not yet."

"Do you think she's the one who's dead?"

I didn't miss the hope in his voice. The current Aneiran queen was one of the last witches in the world, a survivor of the bloody Witch War that had torn entire nations down about ten years before Aneira attacked Erenelle. Stories said she was even behind whatever had happened to start the witches fighting each other. Hell, stories said she was a monster. But her vicious magic had been responsible for much of the death and destruction we saw after Aneira declared war on the giants. We'd only caught glimpses of her over the years, mostly at night from a distance, as she never seemed to emerge during the day. But from the way everyone in the capital scattered from her path, fear in every line of their body language, even those brief moments had left me wondering who was the real power behind the Aneiran throne.

"Maybe," I answered. "I wouldn't bank on it, though."

"What do we do?" Byron asked.

I looked away from the mirror. "Do we have enough ore to add to the defenses?"

Byron's worried look deepened. "That last seam was relatively sparse. We could draw on what we have in reserve and add to the defenses we have in place already, but we need to find another vein soon or we'll run out entirely."

I grimaced. I'd suspected as much, but the scholar was

gifted with numbers, among other things. He'd know the count of our supplies down to the last grain.

Bending back down, I studied the troops again. The magic mirror couldn't pierce the protections surrounding the castle to give us a view within, so whatever they were doing in there was anyone's guess. But the troops on the wall were only in defensive positions now, and the gates had yet to open.

Maybe it was an inside job?

I wouldn't bet our lives on it. We'd all had nearly six years of safety up here in the mountains, far from the ruins of the giant kingdom and the Aneiran prisons alike. I didn't want to lose that now.

"Okay," I sighed. "Keep an eye on them. If they look like they're moving this way, we'll draw on the reserves. But I don't want to use up what we've got prematurely, just in case those Aneiran bastards—"

"What?"

I turned to see Roan at the door to the study. Black-haired with eyes that were so dark, the irises disappeared into the pupil and made his gaze like a bottomless void, the man always looked tense and on the edge of retreating, as if he believed that letting you get too close to him could set off an explosion neither you nor he would survive. He was quiet and secretive, even with us—though the gods knew we all had things we struggled to share with anyone, given the trauma of what we'd been through in the war—and he worried constantly about our safety. But like all of us, he was built big, at least from a human perspective. Most "real" giants towered over ten feet tall by the time they were teenagers. We averaged just under seven feet tall even as adults.

And for that, our people had called us "dwarves." Outcasts, unwanted, told in a thousand ways that we would never belong. Roan was the only one of us who'd still been with his family by the time the war came.

He'd lost them all before it ended.

"Did I hear you right?" Every inch of Roan radiated a churning concern that made the air feel charged. "The Aneirans are coming?"

I shook my head. "No."

His dark eyes flashed between me and Byron, wary.

"Someone in the castle is dead," I explained. "A royal. We don't know who. But the soldiers are taking up positions on the walls."

He closed his eyes briefly, his jaw muscles jumping like he was fighting to stay calm. "Anyone heading this way?"

"Not yet," I replied.

Roan didn't look reassured. "I'll check the defenses."

Before I could say a word, he strode away from the study and I heard the front door slam a moment later.

"I'll keep an eye on the ore supplies," Byron offered. "Make sure he doesn't take them all."

"He knows we don't have much from today's finds," I replied. "I saw him reading the reports when you went to put your pickaxe away."

Byron sighed, but he nodded before heading for the door. In his own way, I knew Roan was only trying to protect us. Sure, he took it to a level of damn near paranoia even on a good day, which annoyed some of the others, but I couldn't really fault him for it. Loss could make you obsessed with guarding what little you had left.

And all any of us had these days was this place and each other.

The heavy door swung shut behind Byron. I looked up at the wooden beams of the ceiling. "You good?"

A faint hum carried through the wall nearest to me. Our cabin didn't speak, exactly. But it always made its opinion known.

Satisfied, I wove past the other enormous chairs scattered around the massive study. A few were piled with various momentarily paused projects—a stack of Niko's plant journals, a collection of Roan's woodcarvings—while Lars' bore neatly folded furs and Clay's stood beside a precarious collection of dirty teacups left abandoned. Six of the seats were angled in one way or another toward the fireplace on one side of the room—even Byron's desk, though he was some distance off to better protect his books and projects from any stray embers. Alone on the opposite end of the room, Ozias' seat faced the window, far from the warmth of the fire, looking out instead on the cold, snowy night as if that was the place the enormous man felt he really belonged.

Down the hall, Clay was cracking jokes while his twin brother Lars prepared a late dinner, and my stomach grumbled at the delicious smells carrying from the kitchen. Gods, Lars could cook.

"Hey, uh, Dex?"

I glanced over to see Niko coming down the corridor. Leaner than most of us, he had brown hair that nearly hung over his eyes and his olive-brown hands were stained by dirt from some of the many plants he kept around the cabin. He never stayed away from them long, and thanks to his gifts with nature, they were thriving despite the winter outside. Shy, quiet, and gentle, Niko had never been a soldier. He'd lived in the forest with the healer who'd saved him when he was abandoned as an infant, and if not for the Aneiran army finally finding them—and killing the healer—he'd be in that forest still.

And the gods knew the world would've been better for it. Even if he wasn't a fighter, Niko was as gifted with healing as anyone came, and he'd saved our lives countless times over the years with his poultices and herbal infusions. Without him, any number of injuries could have left us losing limbs from infection.

Niko watched me, wariness in his eyes. "Byron said there was movement around the castle?"

"He saw a—"

"Wait, what about the castle?" Clay leaned his blond head around the doorway to the kitchen. Inside, Lars fell silent.

I hesitated. Of the twins, Lars was the steadier one, optimistic as a sunrise and determined to find the positive in any situation, almost as if his fire-affinity meant he only saw the bright side of things. Even in the darkest days before we fled into the mountains here, he hadn't let the Aneirans rock his optimistic faith that somehow we'd survive.

His brother Clay, though, was as mercurial as the water-affinity that his magic possessed. He'd laugh at Death's own reaper, be stubborn as a two-headed mule, and change his mind at the drop of an axe. The gods only knew how he'd react to word of troop movements at the castle, but the last thing any of us needed was to panic.

Yet, *not* telling him or the others what we'd seen would only lead to speculation, which was probably why the infinitely logical Byron had said something in the first place.

Bracing myself, I explained what I'd already told Roan.

Lars shrugged after I finished. "That doesn't necessarily mean they'll come this way," he said, wiping the flour from his large hands with a towel. "Maybe they already know who did it, and they're just being cautious."

"Yeah," Clay agreed, his blue eyes flashing with vicious mirth. "Those pipsqueak bastards love to take their little swords out for a spin."

"Which is why we're not panicking," I said. "We're just—"

The door to the cellar opened. Ozias emerged, his massive axe and broadsword both strapped to his back. His long brown beard and disheveled hair made him look like a wild creature, and the furs and leather gear he wore only added to the image. From what we'd gathered, he was a little over three and a half decades old, which would make him roughly my age, and like Niko, he'd grown up in the forests of Erenelle after being abandoned there as a child.

Unlike Niko, he'd never been taken in by anyone, and the gods themselves only knew how he'd survived. We'd found him several years after the war started—or, really, he'd found us. He'd lurked beyond the light of our campfire at night, watching from the shadows and disappearing like a ghost when we came close. If not for Niko's affinity to nature and the wild telling him the man wasn't a threat to us, we would have thought him an Aneiran spy. But as it was, Ozias had trailed us for months while we traveled away from the war zone before he finally set foot in our camp. For a long time, we'd been uncertain if he knew any language at all, and now if he ever did speak, it was straight to the point and blunt as hell.

For a moment, he paused in the cellar doorway, surveying us all with an inscrutable expression.

"We're not sure there's a threat to us yet," I told him, not even bothering to ask how he'd overheard us all the way from his room in the basement. The earth itself spoke to the man. It would've been useless to try keeping something like this secret.

His dark gaze landed on me, intense and unblinking, more like a predator than a man. But after all this time, I was used to it. He wouldn't attack us.

It was the rest of the world that needed to worry.

Without a word, he turned and strode toward the door, disappearing silently into the night moments later.

"Well, that'll go great for any Aneiran bastards who think they're going to head this way," Clay remarked dryly. "Niko, you good for moving some earth to help him bury a body or twenty?"

Niko shifted his weight uncomfortably, avoiding everyone's gaze.

I threw Clay an exasperated look. I'd never been an officer in the army, but I often wondered if any of my former commanders had felt like they were riding herd on cats some days.

The gods knew I did.

"We haven't needed to bury a body in nearly five years," I said. "And Ozias won't put us at risk."

As long as he didn't get carried away.

Filing that on the list of Things I'd Give a Shit About Only If Necessary, I focused back on the situation at hand. "We'll add to the defenses, and tomorrow, we'll head for the other part of that cavern we found today. With any luck, that's where we'll locate another seam."

Niko nodded quickly, as if holding onto the words. Lars looked more hopeful, but then, nothing much ever dimmed his optimism. And Clay just frowned.

"Trust me," I assured them. "By the time we're done, the magical barrier around this place will be so strong, not a soul on this earth will be able to get in."

5
GWYNEIRA

I had to be dreaming. The cold stone beneath me, the bitter chill on the air... it couldn't be happening. Huddled in the corner of the cell in my beautiful red dress, I hugged my legs to my chest and tried not to breathe the air that stank of urine and far worse things.

Hours had gone by. Maybe more. The time was impossible to tell down here in the darkness, where the bitter chill of oncoming winter seeped through the stones to fill the shadows with skittering sounds and icy fingers that brushed my spine. Wood paneling blocked any view through the window high on the wall, but still I'd heard the sounds of boots, hundreds of them, and shouts of orders as well. The palace guard, moving into position along the walls.

In case I had allies.

In case I'd sold out my country too.

I buried my face in my knees. This *couldn't* be happening. In a moment, only a moment now, I'd wake up and Father would be alive and I'd realize I only had too much to drink at the party, nothing more. And we'd laugh about the little birds who echoed secrets from the walls, and he'd tell me all the ways he planned to protect our home.

And everything would be okay.

A clank from beyond the cell brought my head up. At the end of the corridor ahead, Harran clutched a torch. He eyed the hall outside before shutting the door behind him and then hurrying toward me.

I pushed to my feet, my muscles stiff after so many hours. Against my throat, the red ruby necklace remained like a ball of ice, though whatever choking power it possessed had faded over however long I'd been in this cell.

Not that my renewed cries of innocence had accomplished much, ringing uselessly from the uncaring stone walls.

"My lady." He gripped the bars, staring at me with more fear in his eyes than I'd ever seen. Where normally his carefully brushed hair never had a thinning strand out of place, now the graying hairs were wildly disheveled. "How do you fare?"

"What's happening, Harran? I *swear* to you, Fironia is lying. My stepmother gave me that bottle. I didn't—"

"Shh." He threw another look over his shoulder swiftly. "Fironia is gone, my lady. Leapt from the tower. Her body was found not one hour ago."

I stared at him, unable to process the information. Fironia... was dead?

"Tell me, my lady. Was she the one who gave you the poison? Did she assist you in this? She left a note to say her guilt was too great, and she could no longer live with it. Please, for her sake, tell me the truth."

I couldn't find words, but then through the horror, a memory made itself known. "She left a note? Harran, Fironia couldn't read, much less write. I'd promised to teach her. How could she leave a note if—"

Another clank came from the door, and suddenly, Harran straightened, his face going still and blank. As if on command, he moved aside, staring blankly at the far wall of a cell nearby.

A chill crept over me. His face looked like Fironia's had in those moments after Stepmother whispered to her.

What was happening here?

The door to the dungeon swung open, and my step-mother passed through the opening. Behind her, a servant with their head bowed and an enormous man in leather and fur followed. A chill rolled through me. A Huntsman. Brutal predators sworn to serve their masters without fail, I'd never so much as seen one crack a smile, and even the other soldiers seemed to stay far clear of them.

A folded stack of clothing and a torch were clutched in the servant's hands, while the Huntsman had an axe and a sword slung crosswise over his back. In silence, the servant lit the sconces along the wall and then hurried to stand behind Melisandre again.

On trembling legs, I made myself walk toward the bars. "What have you done to him?" I jerked my head toward Harran, keeping my eyes on my stepmother and not the brutal killer at her side. "What did you do to poor Fironia?"

Melisandre's lips curled. "Leave those." She nodded her head to the servant behind her. The young woman set the pile of fabric near the base of the bars and then retreated. "Now go. You as well, steward."

Harran turned without a word and followed the servant as she scurried from the dungeon like a mouse frightened of a snare.

"Get dressed," Melisandre ordered.

"What?"

She scoffed lightly. "You don't think I'm going to let you be executed in that gown, do you? I might wish to wear it myself someday."

I looked from her to the pile of ratty fabric and back.

"Now. Or my Huntsman will butcher you right here."

The enormous man showed no reaction to the words, his hands clasped in front of him in the parade rest stance I'd seen my father's soldiers take when awaiting his next command.

At the thought of my father, a sob returned to my throat even as anger began a steady boil inside me. Bending swiftly, I snatched the pile from the ground and unfolded it. A rough dress unfurled in front of me, the white panels stained with myriad splotches of brown, and the once-blue trim now ragged. Holes peppered the cloth where seams had torn or mice and moths had eaten their fill. The fabric itself was threadbare, worn thin by a hundred washings.

"If you're done admiring your funeral garb..." Melisandre said.

"Turn your backs," I retorted, my voice thick with rage.

"The dead have no modesty, my dear."

I looked up at her again, seething. "Then you will have to kill me as a princess and be done with it. For while I live, I will not bare myself to anyone when it is not my choice."

Cold contempt twisted her lip. With one finger, she made an upward slashing gesture, and suddenly, pain lanced up my spine like someone had taken a knife to my skin.

The gown loosened and fell around me, all the laces sliced in two, while the ruby pendant clattered to the stone floor, its chain cut. Gasping, I dropped the ragged dress and grasped at the falling fabric, clutching it to my breasts.

"Now, as I said. Put that on."

Hot blood trickled down my spine. Pain pulsed through my skin with every heartbeat. Unsteady breaths left me, and my eyes flashed to the Huntsman.

His face like stone, he didn't take his eyes from the wall beyond me.

Trembling, I bent again and retrieved the ragged dress from the ground. She'd never used magic so openly around me, and my proximity to it now made my skin crawl. In the swiftest motions I could manage, I abandoned the red gown and pulled on the white one, a hiss of pain escaping me as the rough fabric grated over my back.

The cold smile never left Melisandre's face. "Huntsman, take this child and rid her from me. I am sick of the sight of her."

"Stepmother—"

"Take her beyond the Warden Wall and into the mountains."

Horror shot through my veins like icy lightning. The gods themselves only knew what was out there. Wild magic. Monsters. Whole kingdoms that had been swallowed by both.

Melisandre's cold smile grew as if she enjoyed the sight of my fear. "Drag her past where even the bravest hunter dares venture, and there I wish you to cut out her heart and bring it back to me as proof the deed is done."

I gasped.

"Never fear, Gwyneira. You will not need it when you return to me."

Confusion joined my horror, but before I could say a

word, she gestured to the lock and the mechanism undid itself with a clank. The door swung wide of its own accord, and instantly, the Huntsman moved toward me.

I retreated. "What do you mean? You can't do this. You can't—"

She chuckled. "My dear child, once you have been turned, there will be no end to what I can do."

Sharp brambles sliced at my feet and cold snow bit at my skin as the Huntsman dragged me through the woods. Not a servant had looked at me as he took me from the castle. Not a guard or citizen had moved to stop him while he hauled me past the gates, through the city, and all the way beyond the Warden Wall. Every single person I'd known all my life ignored my cries, turning their faces away as if ashamed to have ever laid eyes upon me.

And now there were only the wintry woods, the frozen mountain, and the Huntsman with his unyielding grip on my arm and his ears seeming deaf to my pleas.

"You don't have to do this," I begged, gasping against the bitterly cold air. Through gaps in the trees behind me, I could see the city of Lumilia far below, shining like a snowy jewel beneath the bright sun, the vast lake beyond it like a glistening blanket of light. What had been the entirety of my world now looked as distant to me as the moon.

"I won't go back," I pled, my heart aching at my words. "Please."

He continued on, his granite visage unchanged.

"She's lying. I would never have hurt my father. *Please!*"

Only the crack of the icy terrain and shattering branches answered me.

Onward he climbed, paying no mind to how my cries reduced to whimpers as time dragged on. My feet had grown numb and dead from the cold, and my lungs felt like razors were embedded inside them. The view of Lumilia fell away, blocked by the mountainside and the endlessly white winter sky, and still he continued on until the bright morning sun rose high overhead and I couldn't even hear the crack of snow over the pulsing of my own blood in my ears.

"Please," I whispered.

He gave no sign of hearing me.

"Please, don't do this."

My body tingled, strangely hot, as if the winter had started to burn. Above the pounding of my blood in my ears, ringing like wind chimes rose and fell like waves on the lake. They almost seemed to speak, nonsensically babbling to me like children playing a game.

I struggled to focus past them. "Please, spare me."

The Huntsman's footsteps hesitated for a moment and then continued.

"*Please*. I beg you."

He paused, and I felt him turn as if looking down at me.

"I'm not a killer," I sobbed. "Please."

His hand loosened, dropping me to the snow. Like a sack of flour, I flopped against the earth, the bitter snow around me sinking into the thin covering of my ragged dress. With limbs as unsteady as a newborn calf's, I struggled to push myself up.

Only inches beyond where I lay, the ground ended in a sharp cliff, and my stomach lurched. I had tumbled onto an outcropping of stone, and a great gulf of air opened up below me, the distance playing tricks on my eyes. A thread of dark silver cut through the snowy landscape below, and my breath caught when I realized it was a river. Tiny homesteads no larger than crafted miniatures dotted the expanse while cold and sheer mountains rose all around, surrounding them like the sides of a steep bowl.

I turned back to the Huntsman to find him regarding me.

In a smooth motion, he drew his axe. I gasped, looking around frantically, but there was only air at my back and sides.

"P-please," I begged. "Mercy, please. I'll go. You don't have to—"

"What good would that do? You'll still freeze." With both hands, he clasped the axe in front of him. "In truth, you should have already."

I scooted back on instinct, only to stop in a panic as my hand slipped at the edge of the cliff. "But I didn't. So you don't know that I would—"

"I do. Many a man has frozen himself to death far below the height we are at now. I thought to let you pass into unconsciousness from the cold before I took your heart as her majesty has ordered. But still you are here, even in such a dress as that. So now we must have an end to it." He shook his head. "You plead for mercy, child. That is what my axe brings. I will make it swift."

"No, please." My body wanted to retreat, and I barely kept myself from doing so. "I don't want to die like this. If you have any kindness in you, please. Let my end be of my choosing."

He drew a slow breath, his eyes moving over the empty air behind me and the cold world of winter below.

"It would be mercy for me to kill you now." He hefted the axe.

"No!" I cried, desperation feeling as if it thrummed through every cell of my body.

He paused, the axe suspended in his grip, ready to fall.

"Please, no," I whispered, trembling all over from the frantic need for him to stop. My whole body felt hot, as if my blood was on fire with pure panic to survive. "Let me leave. Please."

And a breath left him. Slowly, the axe lowered back to his side.

"Just let me go. Tell her… anything. Give her an animal's heart in my place. But let me live."

He surveyed the mountains beyond me, saying nothing, and I waited, breathless. No Huntsman would disobey his orders. I was asking the mountain to move itself to spare me.

But then he put the axe away. "The *cold* is not kind, miss, and neither are the Wild Lands that lay only a score of miles from where we stand. Out there you will find yourself wishing you'd let me bring your end quickly."

I didn't answer, using the slight reprieve to try to move away from the cliff. My numb limbs took a moment to respond, doubly frozen by shock as they were. Unsteadily, I crawled, not trusting myself to stand so close lest my wobbling legs sent me teetering into the abyss. Bracing myself on a nearby rock, I pulled myself up, half expecting the Huntsman to change his mind and strike me down where I stood.

"That direction leads away from the castle." He nodded toward the forest to the left of the outcropping where we now stood. "But know that there is nothing out there except mountains and endless snow. It has been decades since summer came to these slopes."

I managed a nod. My feet burning beneath me, I stumbled in the direction he'd indicated.

"I will tell the queen you are dead, Princess," the Huntsman continued. "And give her an animal's heart in your place, as you say. But you must never return."

I looked back at him, my entire body shaking. "Thank you."

His face grim, he nodded.

Hugging my arms to my chest against the cold, I staggered away into the woods.

6

MELISANDRE

A rumble carried through the castle, so strong that cries of alarm rose from the servants as the floors and walls shivered.

My lips curled. It was done. The cursed castle bemoaned the loss of its princess, now almost certainly lying dead somewhere upon the snow. It would take time before she rose again, but compared to the nineteen years of her life I'd been subjected to, that short wait would be nothing. She would return, helpless against my call, and here on the stones where her mother once lay dying, the ravenous beings I'd bartered with for my power would finally be appeased.

I let one hand trail perilously close to the gilded frame as I relished the quaking of the petulant building around me. The Voidborn slid like shadowy eels beneath the glassy surface, but for the first time in nearly two decades, they made no attempt to reach for me.

They could feel a greater sacrifice coming.

Chuckling to myself, I walked to the window as a call

rose from the courtyard. The Huntsman, now returned, a bloody sack in his grip. That must be what set off the castle, sentimental structure that it was. Her blood, perhaps, dripping onto its stones. Her heart, rendered motionless at last in that stained leather bag.

How this miserable building must hate that.

My fangs extended briefly, and I fought the urge to snarl in victory at the accursed castle. Someone might see. Besides, it was enough that I'd won, and that this ridiculous place had been helpless to stop me.

I closed my eyes, willing myself to calm down and resume human form. There would come a day when the world saw my true face, but it was not yet this one.

"Bring me the Huntsman," I called to the guards by the stairs.

They nodded, and one of them raced off to do my bidding.

In the corner, a shadow stirred. One of my servants, contained by the sunlight. Of them all, only I knew the secret of how to resist the sun's burn, but it was never a sure thing. Even I had to be cautious.

The woman's voice was so soft, the guards couldn't possibly hear it. "Your servants await your command, Mistress."

I smiled. Everything hinged on the moment Gwyneira returned, on the culmination of all these years of waiting for when she'd finally be fed to the Voidborn in my place. Then, with the price of my power paid, I'd be free to rule openly, not restrained by the shackles of the creatures with whom I'd bargained for this gift.

Then the kingdom would truly be mine, becoming a land of

night and cold, unafraid of death because we'd already escaped its clutches. Let my sisters worry over their own vows to those beings. If they did not save themselves, I would use my power to take over Gentresqua and every other petty nation, and if they did not bow, I'd wipe them from the face of the earth.

My world would be made only of vampire and prey.

Footsteps came from the hall, and then a knock sounded on my door.

I smoothed the smile from my face. "Enter."

The Voidborn rolled beneath the surface of the mirror as the door swung open, but I wasn't concerned. Only someone with magic in their veins would see anything there at all. And indeed, the Huntsman showed no sign of noticing the seething, hungry creatures whispering at the sight of the blood dripping from the bag onto the stones.

But the castle noticed. Another tremor ran through the stones and I smiled, imagining how this pathetic place would wail if it had a voice.

"The girl's heart, Mistress." The massive man kneeled just inside the doorway and extended the bag to me.

I approached him, fighting back a growl at the scent of blood on the air. Carefully, I took the bag from him, lifting it and catching a drop of blood. The Huntsman's head remained bowed, and surreptitiously I licked the red droplet from my fingertip.

And I froze.

"What is this?" I whispered.

"It is what you requested, Mistress."

"Liar."

Rage curled my fist tighter around the bag. At my back, the creatures in the mirror began to churn.

The man tensed, lifting his head. A trace of a growl escaped me to see how he didn't deny it.

"Where is the girl?"

"Dead in the snow, Mistress."

I sent him toppling to the side as I backhanded him. "Where *is* she?"

"On the mountain."

My fangs extended, and with a sharp motion, I let my magic slam the door. The Huntsman's eyes went wide at the sight of my true face, and in spite of himself, the grown man recoiled in fear.

I was on him in an instant, pinning his enormous form to the ground. My blows struck his face, snapping it back and forth in eruptions of blood.

Murmurs rose behind me. The creatures robbed of their prize were now clamoring to feed.

Because the girl wasn't dead.

My fists slowed. Stuttering breaths left the chest of the Huntsman beneath me. His face was a mess of bruises and blood, already swollen so much that I could barely make out his eyes.

But I couldn't kill him. Not yet.

Disgust rolling through me, I rose to my feet, leaving him on the carpet. Wheezing sounds escaped him as he tried to breathe.

I flicked my fingers at him, and magic twisted through him, binding him to this life no matter what his body looked like now. "You thought to betray me," I said to him. "You will never cease to serve instead. Rise."

Like a poorly designed puppet, the Huntsman climbed to his feet and stood tottering before me.

I licked his blood from my fists, relishing the small meal even if I couldn't gain satisfaction from anything else.

But that would change.

"Now," I said, my skin cleaned enough to fool with the servants in the castle. "You will show my guard where you left the princess—and kill her for certain this time."

7
GWYNEIRA

I ran until I couldn't feel my feet or the ground beneath them. I ran until the air burning in my lungs scraped wet coughs from my throat and blood followed them. Blood followed me everywhere.

Stumbling, I collapsed for the thousandth time to the hard ice and snow. The cold weighed me down, making my limbs like wood. I couldn't even force them to move anymore. Darkness pulled me down, taking me to a world where nothing would hurt and everything would be safe again.

I was so tired. So desperately tired. Maybe if I just lay down for a moment... just a moment...

A warm touch of air drifted over my cheek, gentle and loving like I'd always imagined my mother's hand might have felt.

Not yet... not yet, my precious one...

A shaky breath entered my lungs, and with effort, I pulled my eyes open. Behind me was only snow and a red-splattered trail, already being swallowed by fat flakes drifting down from overhead. My footprints, I realized. My red footprints because my feet were bleeding.

I bit back a sob and turned.

A dream met my eyes.

My cracked lips parted, a faint breath of shock leaving me to puff up like a tiny cloud in the air. The endless sea of evergreen trees around me fell away only a few yards ahead, and a row of stones formed in a line at its end, all of them rough-hewn and about the size of fattened hens. Beyond them lay a clearing, open and flat, a veritable white expanse of snow.

And at its heart...

With arms of clay, I shoved myself to my feet and staggered forward. In three stories of carved wood, the massive cabin stood like a small castle in the clearing. Its center drew up to a point nearly fifty feet high, with intricately whittled gables tracing down either side. The wings of the house extended out, and I counted at least seven tall windows on each floor on both sides. A dark wooden door waited at the center of it all, directly below the peak of the gables three stories above.

Gasping, I stumbled toward it. Everything felt thick, from my body to the air itself, and when I passed the row of stones, a tremor rolled through the earth beneath me, nearly taking me from my feet all over again.

Though it might have just been my own unsteady legs.

But the open space of the clearing energized me—or maybe it was simply hope of being warm again—and as the tremor faded, I staggered onward faster and faster until I reached the door itself. A large brass handle glinted in the light, and above it, a keyhole waited. Fumbling at the handle, I bit back a sob, praying somehow that whoever lived here left it open and that I wouldn't freeze only inches from warmth and safety for want of a key.

The latch gave. I tumbled past the door in a heap of frozen dress and skin.

No shouts rose. I could hear nothing but the pounding of my own blood in my ears, and as I attempted to rise, details made themselves known.

Like the woven rug beneath me. Like the relative warmth of the house ahead, and the smell of coffee and breakfast meats lingering on the air. Someone lived here. Perhaps more than one someone.

"Hello?" I called, my voice rough. I scarcely got the word out before another fit of coughing overtook me. Blood splattered my hand as I covered my mouth, and my lungs ached as if they'd been attacked by a saw. Weakness dragged at my limbs as the coughs subsided, and my body begged me to lie down.

But the winter wind was still licking past the open door behind me.

I pushed to my feet again and maneuvered the door closed. Panting hard against the effort, I turned back and then winced with shame. Specks of blood dotted the rug where my feet had been. No sooner did I enter this stranger's home than I messed up their belongings.

But I couldn't go back outside.

Bracing myself with one hand on the wall, I tried to stay off the rug as I continued deeper into the house, praying all the while that whoever lived here wouldn't have a sword or knife at the ready.

But no one attacked. No one seemed to be home at all.

In a haze of exhaustion, I studied the house. Though the walls were formed of sanded and polished logs, the wood grain had been cut so well it flowed from one beam to the next like a river. Each doorframe I passed was carved in such detail I felt as if I could stare at it for a year and always see something new. The rooms beyond were as massive as the rest of the house, whether I found a library or a workshop. Through a door at the end of the hallway, I spotted a kitchen, and in spite of myself, my stomach growled.

Warmth carried from the room at my side, though.

I turned, peering past the beautifully carved doorframe to see a study easily three times the size of any at the palace. Seven massive chairs of padded leather were set throughout the space, one by itself near the windows to the side and the rest at varying distances from an enormous fireplace. Flames still danced over logs there, sending warmth radiating through the room. I whimpered in pain, my body thawing in tingles and bites.

One of the chairs had blankets stacked on it.

Desperation gripped me. On trembling legs, I wove past the chairs until I reached the one with a pile of neatly folded blankets in varying muted shades. The wool was soft as silk, and I shuddered all over as I wrapped it around my shoulders. The gods themselves must have made this.

I staggered closer to the flames until I couldn't stay on my feet any longer as warmth began to soak into me. Collapsing into a chair with more delicate woodcarvings on a table nearby, I clutched the blanket tightly as shivering overtook me, racking my body like my insides were crumbling. The soft leather padding gave around me, engulfing me as surely as the blanket, coaxing every ounce of exhaustion to overtake my body.

The fire blurred, fading into darkness as my eyes closed and sleep claimed me.

8

ROAN

It didn't matter how reassuring Dex tried to be, by the end of the day it'd become clear there wasn't enough ore in these caves to last us a week, let alone through the coming months.

"We should move on," I said, finally voicing the certainty that had been gnawing at me for hours. "Start exploring the caves deeper in the mountains." The others didn't respond, and I tried not to scowl. "If the Aneirans come this way—"

"We'll be ready, Roan," Dex said. "Even with this, we can—"

The scowl won, and I turned away before the former soldier could finish. I knew what the others thought of me. I was the one who worried. The one who couldn't relax even if there wasn't a trace of threat to be seen. These six men had become like family to me in the decade since we met in the ruins of Erenelle, but they didn't understand. Not really. To be sure, they'd lost people. Buried their dead. Watched our country burn.

But what they *didn't* know was that I was just enough of

an asshole to wish that all those horrors were the only ones I'd seen.

I adjusted the lantern on my helmet, my teeth grinding with frustration. Regardless of what they thought of me, the ore we'd found *wasn't* enough. I respected the intelligence of the men around me enough to believe they knew that. And yes, fine, heading deeper into the mountains was risky. We lived only a few miles from the edge of the Wild Lands, and the damned Witch War had left that territory overrun by the gods knew what. Hell, whole nations had vanished who'd once called those mountains home.

But we needed additional ore, so there wasn't a choice. Not if we wanted to stay safe when the Aneirans came.

Because those bastards would. They always did.

And then people died.

Deep inside, the demon that I kept locked away rolled in its slumber.

I tensed, my hand frozen in midair beside my helmet's lantern light, and it took effort to hold my expression steady as I forced my hand down calmly as if nothing had happened. The sensation of the thing inside me was like a memory of an earthquake beneath my skin, faint but unnerving.

The thing that separated me from any other giant in the world.

The thing that I'd buried over a decade ago, hopefully to never see the light of day again.

And by the gods, at the time, the creature had gone willingly. The shame and horror at what the two of us had done —and what we'd *failed* to do—had been so great it was that or throw ourselves from the nearest cliff. Throughout all the years since, I'd never told another soul what I was, not even the men here. Yes, I trusted Dex and the others with my life. That wasn't the issue. But my truth had never protected anyone.

It only got the people I loved killed.

But lately, the creature had been getting restless—and never more so than in these past few days. The gods only knew why. But for the first time since I buried it, hints of its dreams had started reaching me.

Or, as I would call them, nightmares.

A black-haired young woman dead in the snow. A pain like I'd never known, ripping into my soul. Slithering beings with no eyes and thousands of teeth twisting in the dark, hungry and coming.

Always coming.

I clenched my hand tighter on my pickaxe. The demon had likely gone mad after all these years. Regardless, it wouldn't wake, and it *damn* well wouldn't get out. Not again.

No one else I cared about would suffer because of me.

"There is still the seam to the east," Byron commented, drawing my attention back to the present. He adjusted the lantern on his helmet, scanning the rocky walls around us. "We marked it last week. We can head that way tomorrow and—"

A rumble carried through the earth. All the stone around us groaned as if in pain.

Oh no.

"Ozias!" Dex shouted.

Moving like a force of nature himself, Ozias strode between us and stretched out his hands, bracing them against the walls. His teeth bared amid his beard, making him look like a feral animal. "Move six feet back," he growled. "Now."

The light of our lanterns bounced around while we crowded in together as he'd instructed.

Chunks of rock fell from the ceiling, slamming down on places where we'd been standing. I gripped my axe, useless though it was, and fought to keep the creature inside from waking.

The damn thing would be useless too.

"How're we doing, Oz?" Clay called, watching the ceiling as grit continued to rain down. Dust fogged the air around us, making it hard to breathe.

Ozias grunted. "Tunnel is solid. Shaking will end in—"

He cut off, alarm on his face.

"What is it?" Byron asked.

All around us, the quake stopped. Ignoring it completely, Ozias stared beyond us like he could see straight through the rock.

Which, for him, was basically true.

"What are you picking up?" Dex asked.

"The earth changed."

I stared at him. "It what?"

Without a word, Ozias pushed past us like he was stalking prey.

I watched him go, baffled.

Dex started after him and the others moved to follow. Shaking my head, I did the same, trailing them as they traced a path through the twists and turns deep within the mountain. We'd cut some of these tunnels ourselves, locating the best course by magic, while others were natural cracks in the earth. They were hardly the polished and beautifully formed tunnels found in the mountains of our home country, but we were focused on efficiency, not making something for anyone else to ever see. But after a time, I suddenly realized I wasn't sure when last I'd seen a tunnel we'd personally made.

Wariness rose in me. I wasn't like the others. Yes, I had the innate sense of direction that all giants possessed, even deep within the earth. But I didn't actually *enjoy* being underground. And right now, everything in me wanted to get back to the surface and away from whatever the hell was going on. Our own tunnels had shafts for air circulation. They had backup exits in case we were cut off by a collapse. True, it was rare for a giant-carved tunnel to fall, but stranger things had happened.

Things like this.

"Do, uh, you all recognize anything?" Lars asked.

I glanced over to find the others eyeing the tunnels too. Niko shook his head, nervousness in the motion.

"Hey, Oz," Clay called. "Where the hell are we going?"

The other man didn't respond, continuing to stalk through the halls like he was pursuing a target.

"Fantastic," Clay commented at the lack of answer.

"Air quality still good?" Dex asked Byron.

The academic gave a quick look to the small metal device he had in his hand, and he nodded.

My tense breathing slowed.

Slightly.

Dex motioned for us to keep going. The tunnel followed a seemingly erratic path, curving to the left, veering to the right, always continuing onward but not in a remotely straight line. Beneath our feet, the ground descended one minute and rose the next.

Alarm began to beat a louder drum through me. I had no

idea where we were, and that wasn't normal. Hell, I couldn't tell what *planet* we were on, let alone our location in the tunnels.

And then I rounded a turn to find Ozias stopped before a fissure in the wall.

"What is it?" Dex asked.

Ozias didn't respond.

I craned my neck, eyeing the wall he was studying. The rock was split from the top to the bottom of the tunnel in a jagged line, with the gap nearly three feet wide, but no matter how I tried, from where I stood, I couldn't see if anything was beyond.

Without a word, Ozias adjusted his lantern and edged through the gap.

"Okay, uh…" Clay started. "You want to tell us what the hell you're after, big guy?"

Glints of light reflected on the edges of the fissure.

We all froze.

Clay gave a surprised chuckle. "Fuck, never mind." He hurried forward, his brother on his heels.

I glanced around the tunnel, not moving even as the others hurried to follow the twins. I knew what those reflections looked like, but this was way too suspicious for words.

We needed to be more careful. Evaluate this. *Not* rush headlong into—

"Roan, get your ass in here!" Clay called, excitement in his voice.

"Gods of the stone, you're going to want to see this!" Lars added.

Dammit, they never thought things through.

"Roan!" Dex snapped.

Muttering a curse under my breath, I followed them through the gap.

An enormous cavern waited beyond the opening.

I blinked, taken aback in spite of myself. The rough walls stretched fifty feet above our heads, while the cavern itself extended another several hundred feet ahead and on either side, ending in a second fissure through the wall.

But that wasn't what stopped me. Our lantern lights danced across rich seams of dark silver and gold thicker than our torsos. Twisting through the rock from ground level up to the distant ceiling, they covered the walls like vines embedded in the stone.

"Have you ever seen anything like this?" Niko whispered.

I shook my head while around me, the others did the same.

"How did we not know about it?" Dex asked, glancing at Byron and Ozias. Between the former's calculations and the latter's sense of the earth, we rarely missed an opportunity to find more ore.

Let alone a quantity like *this*...

Byron's brow rose in response to the question, his mouth moving like the normally articulate man was at a loss for words.

"Wasn't here," Ozias supplied.

Everyone turned to him. He was eyeing the stone walls like they'd done something suspicious.

"Earth changed," he continued. "Moved ore through the rock. Gathered it here."

"Is that..." Niko looked at the rest of us like he hoped we had an answer. "Have you ever heard of ore doing that?"

Dex shook his head. "Where are we?"

Glaring at the walls as if daring them to try something, Ozias didn't respond.

Byron tugged out the maps and studied them for a few moments. "If we factor in how far we walked and the trajectory of those tunnels away from the ones we carved, I think we're..." He looked from the paper to the cavern and back, the alarm on his freckled face growing. "Right beneath our house."

My eyes slid up to the ceiling of the enormous cave.

"How is that possible?" Lars asked. "We checked this area years ago. There was ore but nothing like this."

"And nothing like those tunnels either," Clay added.

"Earth changed," Ozias repeated as if annoyed we hadn't listened.

From the corner of my eye, I saw the others glance at each other, but I didn't take my attention from the stone above us. "Could we charge it?"

The men looked over, staring at me.

"Could we?" I asked again, addressing the question to Byron. "Charge the ore here to serve as protection around the house?"

The man's brow shrugged. "Theoretically, though there's still the distance through the rock above us to contend with. By my calculations, there are several hundred feet of stone for the power to pass through, so we would still want to put the ore barrier around the house too—"

"But is it *possible*?" I stressed.

He studied the stone above us a moment longer. "Yes."

I could practically feel the thrill that ran through the room. Niko's mouth split with a grin, while Clay let out a laugh that was pure elation.

"A barrier on the surface around the house would still be

advisable," Byron warned. "To ensure the visual safeguards are secure, disguising the cabin from the sight of anyone in the woods who might try to approach our home. But..." He nodded slowly, as if warming to the idea. "This could supplement that defense with greater power than we've ever had."

"Good enough." Dex adjusted his lantern and then hefted his pickaxe. "Everyone take what you can, and we'll charge the rest before we go."

We all grabbed our axes and headed for the walls.

Several hours later found us hiking back to the surface and through the forest, more ore in our possession than we'd been able to bring in for a long while. Below the cabin, the remaining ore in the cavern practically hummed from the strength of the magic we'd imbued it with, the power emanating out through the stone and into the land around it.

I couldn't help but grin. Fuck the Aneirans. Even the earth itself was aiding us in turning our hideout into a veritable fortress.

"I'll get some of the new stones placed before full dark," Byron said as we passed the ring of ore that defended our clearing. The enormous cabin came into view like a welcoming shadow in the twilight ahead. "If anyone wants to assist..."

He trailed off, stopping in his tracks.

"What is it?" Clay called up to him from the back of our group.

Byron didn't respond. Carefully, we all walked closer, following his gaze toward the clearing.

Smoke rose from the central chimney of the cabin.

"Did any of you leave a fire burning?" Niko asked worriedly.

Noises of negation came from the others in low murmurs. Staring at the cabin, I didn't make a sound. No one should have been able to get past the wall of magic emanating from the stones far beneath us. Not a witch or the queen or the long-since-dead Jeweled Coven themselves.

Dex started toward the house and warily, I followed him. I couldn't see any footprints in the snow, but that wasn't saying much. More had fallen while we were in the tunnels. It easily could have covered the tracks left by an intruder.

Or twenty. Or an army.

Deep within me, the creature stirred, almost as if waking again after all these years. My teeth clenched as I fought it.

Like hell that thing would endanger these men.

But if there were any Aneirans here...

Carefully, I drew out my pickaxe, while all around me, the others gripped their tools as well. With a nod, Dex directed Clay and Lars to the left, Niko and Ozias to the right. Byron and I stayed with him as we approached the house, my ears straining for any sign of Aneirans ripping the place apart inside.

Nothing. Beyond our quiet footsteps, even the faint whisper of snowfall had gone silent. I peered past the frosted windows near the entrance and then shook my head at the others when I saw no sign of movement within.

Dex carefully touched the door handle and then twisted it slowly.

Locked.

That made no sense. Why would the intruder secure the door behind them?

Eyeing the windows, Dex withdrew his key and put it in the lock. My incredulity grew as the door resisted opening for a moment, as if the house wasn't sure it wanted to allow us back inside.

Which was insane. We'd *made* the damn house. Our magic had imbued it with something resembling a mind of its own, but why the hell would it suddenly want to keep us out?

Unless this wasn't the house's doing. Unless it was the queen's magic barring us from entry.

But why claim the house and not capture us?

The demon inside me grumbled louder, rousing a bit, and its hunger for fire and destruction came with it. I breathed slowly, in through my nose and out of my mouth, fighting to keep it asleep.

Dex pushed open the door.

Smudges of dried blood marked the rug and floor inside.

The rumbling grew louder in my mind.

Fuck me, I would be putting *everyone* in danger if I lost control now, not just some damn intruder.

Unaware of the battle I waged with myself, Byron gave a quick hiss to the others and the men returned to the door, their focus on the cabin.

As well it should be. I wasn't going to lose control. I damn well *wasn't*. They'd deal with the intruder, I'd stay fucking Erenlian, and no one would know what I really was.

"Roan?" Niko whispered, his dark eyes trained on me with burgeoning alarm, as if he was picking up something.

Adjusting my grip on my pickaxe, I didn't respond as I forced myself to trail Dex inside. The former soldier was tracking the blood away from the door. The marks continued through the hall, oddly veering wide of the rug except for those first few spots, almost as if the intruder had decided to avoid staining the carpet. And the smears were strange. Small, with no sign of boots or tread.

Barefoot.

And *human*.

My heart began to pound harder. A human was here. In our home. The intruder had gotten past the barrier wall and all the magic we'd poured into the cavern below. They'd even gotten past the house itself, which should have been impossible, and now they were lurking somewhere inside.

Injured. Bleeding.

I squashed the flicker of care that rose inside me. They might be a soldier.

Dex neared the kitchen and then paused to see the steps had doubled back, turning to the study. What had they wanted in there? Byron's magic mirror, perhaps? One of his projects designed for our protection?

At Dex's nod, I pushed the study door aside. Warm air made me blink against its sudden dryness, and the heat began to sap the chill from my mining gear. Someone had built the fire up high in here. Perhaps to burn something of ours?

The bloody footprints continued toward the fireplace and circled to the front of my seat. My heart thudded in my ears, and I couldn't make myself wait for the others any longer. The human had targeted my chair out of all of them. Why?

Did they understand how much of a challenge that was to the possessive monster inside me? Was that their plan?

I'd kill them before I let that thing wake.

Tightening my grip on my pickaxe, I lifted it to strike as I eased around the chair.

And then I froze.

"What by the gods?" Byron murmured behind me.

I couldn't move. Even the demon within me had gone totally still.

It was her. Oh, gods damn me, it was the woman from the demon's dreams, alive and curled in the seat, a blanket wrapped around her. Her black hair was dark like jet stone and entirely a tangled mess. From beneath the edge of the blanket, her ravaged feet stuck out, bare and bloodied. All the rest of her remained hidden beneath the wool, and her eyes were closed.

And she was beautiful. Like morning sunlight through ice. Like a seam of dark spring earth between freshly fallen snow. I'd never seen anyone—hell, *anything*—as mesmerizing.

I shivered, irrational, impossible needs rising in me. I wanted to help her. Heal her. Touch her despite the rough-ness of my hands and the fact I hadn't been gentle with anything other than my wood carvings in over a decade. I couldn't fathom the nightmares the creature had been seeing—her lying dead in the snow, her pale skin even more colorless than it was now—but horror boiled at the edges of my mind at the idea that any of it might come to pass.

My eyes trailed across her red lips, everything in me

filled with the desire to kiss them until she was safe and the world was better for her.

Treluria...

A shudder rocked me as the word rose from the creature deep inside, more emotion than speech.

Nothing else would have brought the surging needs inside me to a jolting stop.

Treluria wasn't real. Not at all, and sure as hell not for me. The whole concept was just a bullshit ploy to make young maidens fall in love with opportunistic men who'd lavish them with gifts and pretend those old stories were real just to get them into bed.

Because the idea that there was some person out there meant for you, destined by the gods or fate or whatever to be yours for all eternity...

Your true love.

I took a step back, as if I could distance myself from the need and desire swirling in my gut like red-hot poison. This was the demon's madness. Finding your treluria was rarer than the most precious gemstone, and it only happened to *real* giants.

Not something like me.

"Is... is she...?" Clay whispered.

Dex reached out only to hesitate for a heartbeat as if concerned what touching her would do, before he carefully pressed his fingers to the side of her neck.

A little gasp entered her lungs, and Dex withdrew his hand instantly. A shudder went through her and she whimpered as if in pain, never opening her eyes.

The tiny sound was like a blade straight into my heart.

"It's a trick," Ozias growled, his voice tight.

"Yeah." Lars gave an unsteady nod. "The queen sent her to tempt us into letting our guard down."

Ozias grunted. "Throw her back into the snow."

"Wait, what?" Lars protested. "I didn't say—"

"Look at her feet," Niko interrupted, staring at her. "Do you think she walked here barefoot through the snow?"

"How could she?" Byron countered, quietly incredulous. "Frostbite would have killed her."

"A witch?" Lars suggested.

Clay nodded. "How else could she make it past the barrier and the locked door?"

"A witch so powerful she could overcome all our spells," Byron pointed out, disbelief in his voice. "But who couldn't conjure herself boots and warm clothing for the snow?"

Their theory weakening, the others hesitated.

"Maybe she doesn't know she's a witch," I murmured.

The men glanced at me. I swallowed dryly, realizing I'd spoken the thought out loud.

Gods, even my control over myself was slipping, to say nothing of the thing inside me.

"Yeah, maybe," Niko agreed, nodding. "But we should help her until we figure it out."

Ozias glared at him. "What if she's Aneiran? She could summon their army. Lock us up." He shook his head. "Throw her out."

"We can't just kill her," Lars protested.

Clay made a hedging noise. "But if she *is* Aneiran—"

"Enough," Dex cut in, taking his eyes from the girl with a sharp breath. "Even if she is, *we* are not. We don't kill people simply for existing, and we don't condemn people for crimes we don't know they've committed. That's the Aneiran way, not ours. Agreed?"

At his pointed glance, I nodded and the others did the same.

Gritting his teeth, Ozias looked away.

"Agreed?" Dex pressed, watching him.

The other man made a grunting sound, jerking his head in acknowledgment.

Dex gave a short nod. "We check the perimeter and we keep watch, but we let the girl stay, at least until we have more information. Clay? Lars?"

The twins tore their gazes from the young woman, and their blue eyes blinked like they'd both been dazzled. "Huh?" Clay asked.

"Confirm the spells outside are still in place."

Both men nodded fast and strode for the door, though I didn't miss how they kept throwing glances back at the young woman in the chair.

"Byron," Dex continued. "Keep an eye to the mirror. See if you can spot anything that'll give us more of a clue to what the hell is going on here."

The scholar gave a quick jerk of his head as well and strode to his desk, swiftly focusing his attention on adjusting the mirror.

My eyes slid back to the young woman. The blanket had slipped from one shoulder, revealing the stained, ragged upper edge of a thin dress that would barely be sufficient in the summer, let alone in the mountains in winter.

"So..." Niko started. "What do we do with her?"

In my chair, the young woman stirred briefly and we all froze. Another frightened whimper escaped her, the sound cutting straight through me. Her brow furrowing tightly, her eyes never opened while she tucked her face closer to the soft leather of my chair.

As if it could protect her.

As if, maybe, I could.

"We should put her in a room upstairs," I said, the words blurting from me. "I can— I mean…"

What was I thinking? To put her in my bed?

My fingers curled, craving that soft skin beneath my touch. My mouth watered, desperate to taste all of her, while my cock ached to take her, to make her fall apart with pleasure. True, I'd never had anyone like that, never trusted myself or the demon inside me enough to sleep with anyone, but with her…

The creature shifted within me.

Mine…

Horror shot through my veins and I retreated a step, nausea rising to take the place of my need. By all the gods, that thing could never claim her. *I* couldn't. Not when I knew what would happen.

I would fail her. Hurt her. Watch her burn and die like so many others, and I knew without question I'd die right along with her, even if only on the inside.

I didn't protect people.

I destroyed them.

"Roan's right."

My eyes snapped to Niko at his words, but his attention was still on the young woman.

"She needs somewhere more comfortable than this," he continued.

Ozias turned away, shaking his head.

"Agreed." Dex stepped forward.

The creature rumbled possessively and I bashed it down with all my might. She was not ours. She could *never* be ours. And regardless, my heart was that of a giant, not a monster. I would never begrudge these men sharing anything I wanted.

Any*one*.

I turned away as Dex lifted her gently from my chair, cradling her like she was made of glass. The others would care for her. Tend to her needs. And I would keep my distance.

For her sake. For mine.

Because no matter what the creature deep inside my mind wanted to dream, no one should ever love something like me.

9
GWYNEIRA

I raced through the palace, calling for my father, but he never answered. The halls threw back my cries, returning them to my ears warped and strange. Thick mist twisted like living tentacles along the walls, choking tight against the stone as if to wring the life from the castle itself, and from all the ceilings, gnarled branches hung down, heavy with apples that dripped with thick red poison.

And blood.

My heart pounded. I couldn't breathe, and I knew someone was chasing me. Melisandre, her cold laugh echoing down the corridors, her icy smile just beyond where I could see. I had to warn my father about her. Had to tell him he was in danger, but I couldn't find him anywhere. The castle walls hid me, twisting and turning to keep me ahead of her reaching grasp, but the castle couldn't last forever. Already the corridors were coming to an end, emptying into a prison cell with thick bars I couldn't escape. Her calls carried down to me, coming closer, taunting me and drawing inward like a snare, and when she found me, a fate so much worse than death would await.

Seven shadows surrounded me.

Peace settled over me like falling snow. Their hands were strong and firm, holding me secure, and they murmured words of concern and comfort that washed away my fear and left only calm. The prison cell faded away, the hard stone melting into soft cotton and carved wood. Warm air brushed my cheek, and a comforting blanket covered my body. Though a pit of cold pain felt lodged in my center, I was safe now, far from my stepmother's grasp, held secure by the seven shadowy figures who would never let me fall.

I opened my eyes.

They weren't a dream.

My breath caught. I lay on a large bed, the mattress firm but not too hard beneath my back. A pillow supported my head and a thick blanket covered me while warm flames danced in a small fireplace on the far side of the room.

But seven men stood in the room with me, and without exception, they stole my breath.

Two were like mirrors of one another, standing on either side of where my head lay, towering over me. Their hair was blond and their eyes were as blue as the summer sky. They had the rugged good looks of some of the farmhands I'd seen come into the castle kitchens from time to time—an air that said they were as comfortable under the bright sun as they were indoors—with square jaws and strong cheekbones, broad shoulders and muscles that bulged from their crossed arms.

Beside them, two more men watched me. One of them looked almost my age, with a youthful face, olive skin, and dark eyes. His hair was as brown as fresh-turned earth, and his features were sharp. He was leaner than the two blond men, and though I'd never call him delicate, there was an energy around him like he could slip through the woods as silently as any forest creature, passing unnoticed between the branches and leaves. The man across from him appeared a bit older, with curls that were as red as copper and freckles across his pale cheeks and nose that stood out, nearly as bright as his hair. He was stockier than the young man, though still as tall as the rest, with an inquisitive look in his brilliantly green eyes like he was analyzing everything in sight.

But the man at the foot of the bed brought my gaze to a halt as firmly as if he'd ordered me to give him my attention. His dark eyes were cold and calculating, a look I'd seen often in the gazes of my father's best generals, and the iron in his bearing only added to the impression. His skin was light brown, and beneath his short dark hair, there was a maturity to his face that made me think he was older than the others, and his jaw was set like stone. His nose was ever so slightly crooked, like maybe it'd been broken at some previous time, but somehow, the flaw only made him look more intimidating. To be held in his focus left me with the feeling that at any moment he could strip me bare and find all my secrets.

My heartbeat accelerated, my breath coming short and fast, yet I wasn't sure it was fear I truly felt. I *should* have. That would be rational. Sane. I was trapped between these enormous strangers, laid out like a sacrifice, and how easy would it be for them to pin me here?

On the bed.

Between them all.

I swallowed dryly. What was this? I'd never had thoughts like this about a single man at court, to say nothing of the irritating royal suitors who thought they could impress me with their mere presence. And yet at the sight of these strangers, a hot sensation twisted in my core, making me ache between my legs. My lips parted, and the general at the foot of the bed snapped his gaze toward the motion.

The ache grew worse, and my legs twitched with the impulse to move apart and invite his attention there too. To let them all touch me as no man ever had.

What was happening to me?

Embarrassment arrived, barely in time to stop me from humiliating myself, and I tore my gaze from him only for it to land on the last two occupants of the room. One stood in the shadows by the door with his body turned partly away from me, whether to hide or to flee, I didn't know. He was lean-built too, but whereas the younger man beside the bed had a gentle fluidity to his bearing, this man looked like a haunting specter of death itself, more at home in a grave-yard than here. His arms weren't crossed, but rather gripped around his middle as if he was trying to hold something inside, and his shoulders were drawn up protectively. His black hair fell around his face, partially hiding his sharp cheekbones and equally sharp jaw, and between the strands, his dark gaze was like an eerie void that darted away from mine the moment our eyes met.

And over by the sole window in the room, the last occupant was the largest of them all, a hulking figure so huge I couldn't fathom how he hadn't drawn my notice until just now. He was larger than a Huntsman, but the bolt of alarm that shot through me at the thought he might be one of them fizzled as quickly as it came. There was a wildness to him, as if the scent of the outdoors clung to him even here. A savagery that even the Huntsmen never possessed. The candle burning on a small table near me couldn't cast light far enough to illuminate every detail of him, but the thin moonlight coming through the window at his back traced him with silver and backlit the edges of his gnarled hair and long beard. He was as still as a statue but with an energy to his muscled form like a predator on the verge of an attack, and even in the shadows, I could see his eyes were trained on me with unblinking intensity.

And he should have frightened me. They all should have.

My body didn't care.

"Who are you?" asked the man who looked like a general.

My eyes snapped back to where he stood at the foot of the bed.

"And why are you here?" added the copper-haired man, his green gaze searching my face like I was a math puzzle he couldn't solve.

I struggled to find my voice. "W-where am I?"

"Our questions first." The order from the general was calm, but it held no possibility of negotiation, like an implacable wall I could beat my fists against, but it would never move.

A growl of agreement came from the enormous man by the window, something cruel in the sound, and when he took a step forward, my heart sped up again.

Gods, he was scarred too. A vicious line ran down one

side of his face, only making him look more dangerous than he already did.

"Who are you?" the general repeated.

I trembled. "I'm..." Doubt assailed me. Should I tell them my name? What if they told the queen I was alive? "No one."

"Throw her out," the scarred man snarled.

Fear gripped me, bringing no traitorous arousal this time, and I pushed back on the bed as if to retreat through the wall and escape the threat.

The bedroom door slammed without anyone touching it.

I froze.

In silence, the seven men turned, staring at the door for a heartbeat. "What the hell?" whispered the blond one to my left, his blue eyes incredulous. "Roan, was that you?"

The man by the door shook his head.

"She *is* a witch," the scarred man snarled.

"I'm not!" I protested. "I've never touched magic in my life."

The blond man's twin made a cautioning sound, clearly disbelieving me. "You got into the house. You really expect us to believe that?"

I stared at him, lost. "I just... I'm sorry. The door was unlocked and—"

Roan's gaze snapped to me. "Liar. I checked it three times before we left."

His dark and bottomless eyes pinned me like knives and then ripped away like he'd torn the weapons from my flesh. I shivered, confused and scared at his vehemence.

"This entire clearing is protected," said the general. "If you got past our defenses, then powerful magic is the only way."

My head shook. "I-I didn't... I was lost in the woods, and then I saw the cabin... and I walked in. Maybe I missed those?"

His eyes narrowed, a look on his face like he couldn't believe what he was hearing. "You saw the cabin. From the woods?"

I nodded.

"Not possible," Roan growled.

My mouth moved, but before I could speak again, the copper-haired man spoke up. "You were barefoot in the snow," he said. "At this altitude, your dress would barely be enough for a summer's day. By all rights, you would have succumbed if you were in that cold for more than a short time. Yet you're here, and your body didn't suffer more than a few wounds and mild frostbite that we were easily able to address. Explain that."

I searched for words but couldn't think of a single thing to say. "I-I just ran. I didn't—"

"From whom?"

Every trace of my arousal had turned to ice, chilled by the threat I could be abandoned once again in the wilderness with nowhere else to go. Yet to tell them the truth could be suicide as well. "Please. I didn't mean to—"

"Answer our questions or go back in the snow," the general said flatly, proving my fears. To look at him, I had no idea if he'd really do it.

The scarred one near the window stepped closer. A low growl left him, and he had a look on his face as if he was already preparing to hoist me bodily from the bed.

Panic propelled my response. "M-my stepmother. I'm running from my stepmother. She..." Gods, maybe I'd already said too much. And if I told them she wanted me dead, they might decide it was in their best interest to give me back so she could succeed in killing me this time. "She wants me gone."

The other men glanced at the general. He was in charge, I suspected. The one they looked to for a plan.

"Your stepmother," he repeated. His attention flashed to the copper-haired man.

For a long moment, the second man studied me, his green eyes narrowing briefly as they scanned over my face, my hair, and the shape of me beneath the blankets.

Quivers spread through me, but not because there was anything erotic in that gaze. Rather, he seemed to be piecing me together like I was an experiment to analyze—one that had given him a result he hadn't expected.

And I couldn't fathom how to predict what conclusion he was drawing.

"The troop movements," he said finally, as if it answered a question.

All around the room, confusion vanished from the men's faces, turning to a dark certainty.

Oh, gods. Even with that tiny bit of information, they had found me out?

"What's your name, woman?" the general demanded.

"Please don't kill me," I whispered.

"Name," he repeated. "Now."

I swallowed hard. I could lie. But would they kill me if they found out I had? Perhaps they'd keep me alive if I told them the truth, maybe in the hope of bargaining with my stepmother. And that might give me a chance to escape.

Though the gods only knew where I'd go.

Another growl came from the scarred man, and it sent

fear flying through my veins like a lightning strike. "Princess Gwyneira of Aneira."

Every man went still.

"Gods be *damned*." Leaning his head back, Roan raked his fingers through his dark hair as if to pull it out. "Is the queen coming? Did you lead her to us?"

"What? No! I—"

"Why are you running from her?" the copper-haired man asked like he was still piecing facts together into a picture, though I couldn't guess what it was. "And what would make you come this high into the mountains to escape her? Surely you had other options."

My head shook again. "Her Huntsman brought me to the mountains. She ordered him to bring me here and kill me because she claims I murdered my father, but I didn't. I *swear* to you, I didn't." I trembled. "The Huntsman let me escape instead."

"*Let* you escape," the general repeated like he didn't believe the words. "Could she be tracking you instead?"

I floundered. "I don't think so. She... she wanted him to bring her my heart." Even now the insane request horrified me. "I begged him to find an animal instead, and he said he would. So hopefully, she'll believe I'm dead." Shivers coursed through me. What was this nightmarish reality, that I was left *hoping* the woman who raised me now thought I was dead?

My shivers grew worse, and no matter how I tried to will them to stop, they continued. "Please. I have nowhere to go, and I'll do anything you ask. Please don't send me away. I beg you."

Several of them looked away as if unable to meet my eyes. The copper-haired man still studied me like I was an enigma while Roan regarded me askance, as if he was waiting for a trap to spring.

And the general glanced at the bedroom door, something thoughtful on his face.

"We can't just abandon her to die," said the younger man by the bedside. He hadn't yet spoken a word, and his voice was soft. His dark eyes watched me with an openness that reminded me of a forest creature. Something wild but thoughtful that would vanish like a ghost if I looked away.

"Niko, this isn't safe," Roan said. "We can't—"

"Then how are we any better than them?" Niko replied.

The other man's face shut down like he'd sealed any trace of reaction inside a stone vault, and he turned away.

My eyes darted between him and Niko. Better than who?

"What's the vote, then?" the general asked the others.

"Let her stay," Niko said immediately.

"Agreed," the copper-haired man said.

The blond twins looked at each other. One lifted his brows at the other, something optimistic and hopeful in his gaze, and the second rolled his eyes in response, his lip twitching like he saw something amusing in his brother's expression. "Stay," they said at the same time.

"Ozias?" asked the general.

The scarred man by the window watched me for a long moment. I felt like a rabbit trapped by the searing stare of a wolf. "Stay," he growled at last.

Raising an eyebrow, the general glanced at the man by the door. "Roan?"

The man's jaw muscles jumped. A heartbeat passed, and when he spoke, he met no one's eyes as he said, "Let her stay." Without another word, Roan yanked open the door and strode out of the room.

The general sighed, but whatever he felt about Roan's behavior, it was buried beneath calm practicality when he turned back to me. "Then it's agreed. If you wish to stay, Princess, you can stay."

Relief stole my breath, even as rationality floundered in the back of my mind. Yes, I had nowhere to go. Yes, my body still heated up every time their eyes landed on me. But these men were strangers. To stay with them... to trust them with my safety...

It was irrelevant. My options were freezing to death or this.

And how alluring was *this?*

With effort, I forced myself to focus. "Thank you."

His head twitched in a nod. "Lars," he said to the twin to my left. "Get her something to eat." His attention flicked to the other twin. "Clay, find her something better to wear. Niko, go after Roan. He's probably checking the defenses again. Help him make sure they're solid." He paused, his gaze still on me. "Though something tells me they will be. Byron, keep an eye on the castle, just in case that Huntsman fails to convince the queen. And Ozias?"

The scarred man's brow twitched up.

"Check the forest. You see any soldiers—or any *Huntsmen*—you take them apart. Understood?"

A satisfied smile curled Ozias' lips, something merciless and deadly in the expression. He nodded.

As the others left the room, the general circled the bed toward me. I tensed.

He sank down on the edge of the mattress and a trace of the tension with which he'd held himself cautiously faded away, almost as if he wasn't sure he should let it go. "I'm Dex."

I swallowed hard. With him closer now, his scent was rich on the air. Warm but with a tang of metal or stone. Its effect on me was sudden, making me flush with heat, and embarrassment rose up quickly on its heels. I'd seen soldiers back home, seen attractive men in the castle, but none had ever impacted me like this. "A-a pleasure to meet you."

"You'll be safe here, Princess. This—" His eyes skimmed over the walls and ceiling. "This place seems to have taken a liking to you."

My brow twitched down. "This place?"

"The house. That door you came through was locked. I know. I locked it myself, and the gods know Roan checked it enough times. But the house..." He glanced around again. "It decided you needed to be let in anyway, I suspect. And that you need to stay." He nodded toward the door.

I shifted uncomfortably in the bed. "So that... that really was magic?"

"Yes."

I trembled.

"Are you not familiar with magic?" he asked, and I had the strangest feeling it was a trick question, like maybe he thought I should be.

"I-I am, but..."

"What?"

I eyed the walls warily. "My stepmother told me I'd go mad if I came in contact with it."

A chuckle left him. "Did she now?"

I looked back at him, confused.

"Princess, that barrier should have killed you on the spot. For pity's sake, we'd just finished reinforcing it to be stronger than ever before."

He paused, his brow twitching down like a new thought occurred to him.

"What?" I asked.

"The earth changed," he murmured.

My wariness increased tenfold. "It did what?"

He looked at me again. "Nothing. But there's no way you should have made it past our defenses, let alone see the cabin within them. If you did, then you have powerful magic inside you."

A nervous chuckle left me, and I shook my head. "No. I don't—"

"We know magic, Princess. Trust me when I say we'd know if there could be any other cause."

I froze. "So... does that mean you and the others have, um..."

"Magic? Yes."

A breath pressed from my chest.

"It's different with each of us. Niko's best with plants and animals. Roan can enchant his art like you wouldn't believe. Byron's amazing with crafting gadgets to use magic. Clay's got an odd sense of humor, so he's often shrinking the beds or playing pranks..." Dex trailed off when he seemed to see how his words were affecting me. I could barely breathe for the thought there was magic all around me. Magic users too. Would I go mad?

Had I already? Perhaps that was the explanation for my attraction to them and the way my body clamored for them to touch me. Gods, even now, my mind was in danger of being swept beneath a flood of fantasies.

Magic was to blame. It had to be.

"Sorry." Dex gave me a polite smile. His gaze flicked down, his hand moving toward mine but then pausing as if he'd stilled the impulse. "Point is, we know what we're doing. You'll be fine."

"And…" I cleared my throat as politely as I could, torn between inching my hand farther away from him and the utterly insane compulsion to reach out and touch him instead. "Which of you made this place? The… the magic here?"

"We built it together."

I trembled, uncertain what to think. Even Melisandre had never displayed such power, though admittedly, she'd hidden her magic work from us all. The gods only knew what she could actually do. But these witches or sorcerers or whoever they were… they'd built a place nearly the size of an entire castle.

And, apparently, it *liked* me.

"You're safe here, Princess," Dex said.

There was something so certain in his voice. So strong, like a solidity that came from understanding the world, when I felt like everything I'd known of life had crumbled in the past day.

I swallowed dryly, wishing I could fall back on that certainty and trust it, if only for a little while.

Dex smiled. It stole my breath all over again.

The bedroom door opened, and the blond one he'd called Clay leaned his head around the opening. Surprise flashed over the man's face at the sight of Dex sitting near me. "I, uh, got some clothes."

I drew in air as Dex rose from the side of the bed and extended a hand to me. Gingerly, I took it, half expecting his touch to shock me. But his palm was warm and dry, and when his fingers closed around mine, his grip was firm.

That strange heat returned to my middle and my cheeks flushed. What would his hands feel like on the rest of me?

Blushing furiously, I looked away only to catch sight of Clay as he stepped into the room. What might his touch feel like too?

"These, uh..." Clay nodded to the clothes in his arms, the pile of fabric looking small compared to how big he was. "I wasn't sure of your size, so if they're too small or if you have trouble keeping them on—" He coughed, his face reddening like an instant sunburn. "I mean, um... I can make more holes in the belt." Looking uncomfortable, he set the clothes on the top of the dresser.

I hesitated, glancing between them when neither moved. Surely, they weren't going to just stand there, watching me undress?

What if they did? And what if then both of them wanted to—

I smashed the thoughts down hard. Magic. This had to be magic, and it was making me insane because this wasn't how reality operated.

And besides, regardless of my attraction to them, it didn't mean they were attracted to me in return. Nor did it mean anything for what could happen if I let any of them know the direction my body wished to take. People didn't share like that. Not in Aneira, anyway. I would surely offend them, or at best, make things incredibly awkward for us all.

And that didn't even bring into it the question of what *I* was thinking to even consider such a thing, when I'd never even been with a man before in my *life*...

The men weren't moving and I didn't know what to do. My fingers reached up of their own accord, brushing the neckline of my ragged dress, and I watched Clay's blue eyes linger on the path my hand had taken.

Did he feel drawn to me too?

"We'll give you a moment," Dex said in a tight voice. Quickly, he turned and pulled open the door. "Clay?"

The other man didn't respond, and Dex snagged his arm, hauling him from the room. The door shut behind them.

A shuddering breath entered my lungs. Madness, all of it.

10

CLAY

Gods help me, I barely made it out of that room.

Dex paced away from the door. "Fuck..." he muttered.

I glanced at him. The former soldier never seemed to lose his composure, but right now he looked like he was keeping it together by willpower alone. Shaking his head as if swearing more inside his mind, he scrubbed a hand over his face and then looked toward me. "'If she has trouble keeping her clothes on'?"

I winced at his dry tone. "*Not* what I meant to say."

"Uh-huh."

"I just—"

"Wanted her too?"

The words brought me up short. "So, you..."

He scoffed, his brow shrugging expressively as he looked away.

So it wasn't just me. Because, gods, when that woman looked at me, it felt like gravity. Like magnetism, pulling me toward her, filling my mind with what it'd be like to run my hands over every inch of her body, to feel her pretty mouth around my cock, or to have her laid out on the bed beneath me, writhing with pleasure as I took her over and over again in every hole she had.

I raked a hand through my hair. I'd been with women in the past. Lars and I had shared plenty. But I'd never felt anything like this in my life. The craving to fuck her until she screamed wasn't even the half of it. When she'd whimpered in her sleep, obviously afraid of something in her dreams, I'd wanted to track down whatever the hell frightened her and make it die.

Was this what finding your treluria felt like?

I tugged my hand away from my scalp, choking on a scoff at myself. Every one of us knew the tales of what happened when male giants found their true love, the one chosen for them by the gods or fate or whatever. The stories said the urge to guard that person with your life and give them anything they needed was overwhelming—as was the need to mate with them, to cement that connection in every way possible. To find your treluria was supposedly rare—like "finding a mountain made of solid gold" rare—but still, the stories persisted.

Because after all, who wouldn't want that? Someone made for you, just as you were made for them? Someone to love for exactly who they were, and who would love you that way too?

Yeah, so it was sappy. Didn't mean it hadn't sounded nice to a kid on the streets, whose own family had kicked him and his twin brother out just for being born "wrong" according to their bigoted asses.

But it was a fantasy. We weren't like ordinary giants. Our prospects had been nonexistent among our own kind, and that was without bringing into it the odds we'd even find someone who drew us that way in the first place.

And now...

I paced away from the door. We'd been isolated for too damn long was all. Or else the gods were laughing hard, bastards that they were, because they'd sent an Aneiran woman who awakened more of a need inside me than I'd ever felt in my life. For all I knew, this was some trick she was playing just to get us to let our guard down.

Dex made an irritated noise and I glanced back at him. The guy was the unofficial leader of our group, and he had legendary self-control.

Right now, he looked a heartbeat away from losing it.

"This has to be a trick," I said. "Magic."

"You saw the girl. She looked horrified at the thought."

"So she's acting."

He gave me a tired look I knew *all* too well.

And I ignored it, same as I always did. "Well, what do *you* believe it is, then?"

He didn't respond.

I glanced toward the stairway, another idea occurring to me. "You think the others..." I tilted my head back toward the bedroom indicatively.

Dex shrugged. "You'd have to ask them."

Yeah, like I was going to have that conversation. Hey guys, I want to fuck that woman until she loses count of her orgasms, how about you? Want to see if she's up for it?

My eyes drifted back toward the door. A shadow moved past the gap at the bottom. Odds were good she was getting naked in there, and damn if that thought didn't fire the blood to my cock.

Gods, I was acting like a teenager. And yeah, okay, so it'd

been a long-ass time since I'd been *around* a woman, let alone slept with one, but seriously, this was ridiculous.

"Well, doesn't matter anyway," I said, trying to push the thought from my mind.

Dex gave me a questioning look.

"She's Aneiran."

His brow twitched up like I wasn't making sense.

"They aren't like our people. There's no chance she'd consider being with two of us, let alone all—"

He made a rough sound. "*She* just survived frostbite that should have killed her, and apparently a Huntsman who should have done the same. We're not propositioning a princess, *especially* an Aneiran one."

"Wasn't suggesting it."

"Yes, you were. Keep it in your pants."

I spread my hands, my temper flaring. "Do you see me going in there?"

A heartbeat passed, and then he grimaced, looking away. "Sorry."

He sounded resigned, and he shifted his weight as if putting more distance between himself and the door.

My temper faded. I'd bet good coin he was fighting to keep from heading back into that room too, and damn if that probably wasn't making him irritable. "It's all right."

"We keep any attraction to ourselves, and we keep the girl safe until we can relocate her elsewhere. That's all. Understood?"

I couldn't help myself. I had to ask. "And if *she* suggests anything?"

Dex's eyes flicked toward the room and then away. "She won't."

Without another word, he headed for the stairs, moving fast.

I sighed, tempted to do the same because there was nothing to be gained hanging around the room of the hot girl who would *definitely* turn us all down—or, more likely, run screaming at the idea.

Erenlians had always bonded with multiple mates, but human society wasn't like ours. Sure, there were a few nations among them—Gentresqua, a couple others—who turned a blind eye to such practices, but plenty more made it *abundantly* clear they opposed the idea among their own people.

Including Aneira.

And that wasn't even bringing into it the entirely *non-sexual* issues at stake—namely, that she was the daughter of the king who'd imprisoned our people. Once she realized who we were, we all could be screwed.

Dex was right. Keeping our distance was the only solution.

The door opened beside me, jolting me from my thoughts, and I scrambled to push the frustration from my expression. Looking slightly nervous, Gwyneira peered past the opening.

"Excuse me?" Her voice was hesitant.

"Yes, Princess?"

"C-could you help me with the, um..." Her cheeks flushed pink, and the traitorous, ludicrous thought of what *else* I could do to bring such color to them raced through my mind. "The laces of this vest are just a bit hard to reach. Would you mind assisting me, please?"

Words fled, and the gods themselves were the only ones with a clue what they would've been. My mouth moved for a moment, hunting for a way to tell her it would be best if I didn't, but all that blurted from my lips was a tight "Sure thing" before speech abandoned me again.

She stepped back, making space at the door. I froze for a moment, but what was I supposed to do? Run from her like I was deranged?

We needed to keep her calm. Happy. *Not* inclined to bring the Aneiran army here to lock us all up.

Though, really, she probably wouldn't. If her story was true, they'd lock her up too.

Breathing slow and steady, I walked inside, carefully keeping my eyes damn near aimed at the ceiling when my path took me close to where she stood. But my careful breathing didn't help when I caught her scent on the air.

Gods *save* me. A hint of winter's chill, undercut by traces of roses and apples and citrus too, and it all threatened to weaken my knees. I made myself keep walking, putting several more feet of distance between us for both our sakes. Her dress lay at the foot of the bed, the worn fabric barely usable for rags, let alone clothes. Breeches covered her legs now, the clothing a tad too big but still useable. I'd conjured them in a hurry, and stolen a few things that had shrunk in the wash besides, but though the fabric was a bit baggy, it still didn't fully disguise her form.

And damn, oh damn, what a form it was...

I swallowed hard, trying to stop myself from staring at her. A shirt of white cotton hung from her shoulders, the top gaping open for several inches below her collarbones, offering a tantalizing hint of the soft mounds that lay below, while a brown leather vest was wrapped around her chest, solid in the front but hanging in loose laces below the ebony waves of her hair on her back. Baggy or not, the pants still couldn't hide the curve of her hips and the lusciousness of her ass before continuing down her beautiful legs to where her bare feet were wrapped in bandages.

She turned her back and looked at me over her shoulder. "Do you, um, need me to bend over a bit, or...?"

Gods of the Stone, this was going to kill me. "No, this is fine." I swallowed down anything else I might have said, idiotic as it *definitely* would have been. Breathing carefully, I took up the laces and began pulling them tighter.

My tug on the laces drew her ass closer to my cock, and I bit back a groan. Much more of this and I was going to make a fool of myself—or worse, terrify Gwyneira. I wouldn't hurt her or make a move without her consent, of course. But if she'd give it, I'd have her moaning with pleasure as I thrust my cock deep into—

"Is something wrong?" Gwyneira asked, starting to pull away from me.

The motion snapped me back to reality. "Nope, everything's fine."

She paused as if hearing something in my voice, and quickly, I set to finishing up the laces before taking a large step back from her. "There," I said. "How's that?"

Turning, she pushed on the vest a bit, causing her breasts to move beneath the leather. "Good, I think. Thank you."

Afraid my voice would betray me, I could only nod.

"So what may we do now?" Gwyneira prompted, taking a step toward me.

Yep, this would *definitely* kill me. "I could show you the rest of the house?" I managed to say.

Trepidation flashed over her face. She glanced at the walls like she was worried they'd sprout thorns, but after a moment, she nodded. Making myself turn, I gestured for her to lead the way out the door, and I fought to keep my eyes from her ass as she went.

"Stairs to your left," I said.

She headed in that direction, eyeing the corridor around her, and staying firmly to the middle of the hallway and weaving around any furniture there as if keeping as far from it all as she could.

Curiosity rose in me. "Everything okay, Princess?"

Gwyneira hesitated, not quite looking at me. "It... it's a lovely house. Very lovely."

She sounded like she was trying to pacify an attack dog.

My brow furrowed as I followed her down the stairs. Why would she be afraid of the house? It had let her in, hadn't it? Insisted she stay too. Why would she be concerned about it now?

Unless she planned on betraying us. Unless she worried it would hurt her when the truth came out.

I scrubbed a hand over my face. I felt like a toy in a child's game of tug-of-war, yanked endlessly between two extremes. I wanted her. I was wary of her. Back and forth, back and forth.

But something inside me was bothered by her dislike of the house, and not for any reason to do with her potential betrayal. Part of me wanted her to like the home we'd built. Wanted her to feel safe here. We'd raised the structure six years ago, Niko's magic pushing back the trees and under-brush while the rest of us drew the building from the earth. Lars' gifts with fire added twists and turns in the chimneys and walls that let only a few fireplaces keep every room warm. My own gifts with water added plumbing better than anything the humans possessed. Roan shaped the halls with his woodcraft while Byron fashioned undying lanterns from otherwise ordinary metal and minerals. While Ozias had formed the portions belowground, his gifts with the earth creating a foundation for us that would stand the test of any threat or winter storm, Dex had reinforced the layout aboveground to do the same. But between us all, our magic had given this place a life of its own.

And now the place was a fortress and a guard dog, all rolled into one. It'd do its damnedest to protect us, and now that *us* included her.

But... was I certain it did?

Gwyneira left the steps and glanced toward me, a question clear in her eyes.

I shoved my apprehension aside, putting a friendly expression on my face as best I could. "The kitchen's straight ahead. Study's to the left where you, um..."

"Passed out?" She flashed me a nervous smile with a hint of humor, and my heart tripped over itself.

"Uh, right. Well, you're welcome in there. We can get you a chair or—" I cut off, hitting the brakes on making an idiot of myself. "Or whatever. There're other rooms too. I can show you those, or would you like some food first?"

Lars poked his head around the kitchen door. "I have snacks ready."

Gwyneira smiled. "Food would be lovely, thank you."

I'd swear my twin brother's face started to turn red at the sight of that smile, but he ducked back too quickly for me to be sure. "This way, then." I gestured for her to go ahead of me.

At the end of the hall, Niko appeared. "Everything all right?" His eyes went straight past me to Gwyneira.

Byron emerged from the study. "Did I hear mention of food?"

When the princess hesitated, I answered. "Yeah. Weren't you watching the magic mirror?"

He shrugged. "Dex wanted to keep an eye on it for a bit."

The academic was barely looking at me, all his attention on the princess as he gestured for her to continue down the hall. Niko instantly headed that way as well.

Gods help us, were they all going to crowd into the kitchen?

It certainly looked like they were going to try.

Gwyneira stopped just past the entry. "Oh my."

I followed her gaze and then suppressed a scoff. Clearly my brother was taken with her. Trays of every kind of food imaginable covered the table. Fruits, vegetables, sweets, and pastries. Meats already sliced and more still on the roast. Breads in a basket and soup in a pot. My eyes slid to Lars, finding his focus locked on Gwyneira.

"Snacks," I repeated dryly.

He shrugged, still watching her. "I thought she might be hungry."

"Right."

"You did all this?" the princess asked.

Lars nodded.

Her smile was becoming more nervous by the second. "Forgive me, but... is it magic?"

I gave her a confused look.

"Ah, yes, Dex mentioned that." Byron directed his words to the rest of us. "She's a bit... *concerned* about magic."

Understanding dawned on the faces of the others while I glanced at the princess. Was that why she'd looked uncomfortable about the house? But what would she think about the clothes she was wearing? Damn near everything around us had magic involved somehow.

My brother smiled. "I promise you, it's quite safe. I make food for us all the time."

I scoffed. "Not this nice, you don't."

He ignored me.

"Magic won't hurt you, Princess," Niko reassured her. Fishing in his pocket briefly, he drew out a fragment of a twig. He always carried things like that, whether it was sticks or leaves or seeds. In his palm, the wood sprouted small branches that erupted in clusters of pinkish-white flowers. Still smiling, he extended it to her, the twig having become a miniature bouquet.

Yep, for sure I could add that one to the "enamored of her" camp. At this point, Ozias and Roan were probably the only ones who weren't.

Staring at Niko, she was motionless for a moment, her mouth a tiny *O*. Her eyes darted to the magical creation.

I held my breath, hoping for his sake she would take the small gift. Niko was notoriously shy, owing to a childhood growing up away from everyone but the healer who'd saved him when he was abandoned in the forest. His heart was also about as big as the mountain itself, and he'd saved our lives more than once with his magic when we were hiding from the Aneirans in the woods. If she refused his gift, I knew it would hurt him.

And maybe she concluded the same thing because after a heartbeat, she reached out with a trembling hand, taking the flowers. "Th-thank you. They're beautiful."

His smile broadened, and I exhaled with relief.

"How is it..." She hesitated as if uncertain what to say. "I mean to say"—she cast the table an uncomfortable look—"how can food be made by magic and still be *food*?"

My brother shrugged. "Replication spells. A few stasis spells to keep things fresh so I have them to copy. We have a fairly substantial pantry, so it gives me a lot to work from. My gifts tend toward fire, so cooking things is easy."

Gwyneira's eyes were big as saucers.

"Maybe we should try a few dishes?" I offered. "Show you they're safe?"

Relief flickered across her face. She nodded.

With a gentlemanly bow, Lars extended a hand to her and, carefully, she placed her fingers on his palm. I followed as he led her to the table, shaking my head at his back.

And the guys all liked to claim *I* was the show-off.

She sank onto the bench, watching the food in front of her like she half expected it to come to life and bite her. I sat down next to her while Lars took her other side. "What would you like us to try for you?" I asked her.

"Um..." She pointed to one of the strawberries.

Lars immediately snagged a strawberry, swallowed it down quickly, and then took up another, offering it to her. She hesitated and then leaned over and took a bite straight from between his fingers.

Oh, sweet gods, this girl was going to kill us all.

I fought back the urge to adjust my hardening cock, and I would swear Lars held his friendly smile in place by willpower alone.

By the door, Niko cleared his throat. "So, uh, Princess?"

Byron's green eyes widened and he shook his head at Niko, a tiny motion that I could read loud and clear. We didn't need anyone propositioning her this second. Or at all. There were still the issues of Aneira, our people's imprisonment, and what she'd do if she found out who we were. Hell, there was also how she'd most likely panic if we let on how different our customs were from anything she knew.

Niko didn't take his eyes from Gwyneira. "What would you like to do after dinner?"

I'd swear everyone in the room stopped breathing.

"Like, see the house or the grounds or something?" he continued quickly, as if realizing what he might've implied.

"Well, I..." Gwyneira's face was slightly pink, as if she'd started to blush and the reaction hadn't quite faded. "I'd like to know what I can do to help all of you."

Oh, *definitely* no one was breathing now.

"What do you mean?" I managed to ask.

"You're giving me a place to stay. Your food. Clothing. How can I repay this?" A hint of pain flickered through her expression, bringing everything else I was feeling to a halt. "I don't have any gold or jewels. Any lands to offer or... anything."

The others glanced around the table, discomfited at the sight of her pain.

"You could help us," Niko offered kindly.

She looked at him with confusion, and I wasn't far behind. What was he thinking? Bring her to the mines?

"We're gone most of the day," he continued. "And having someone keep an eye on the house in case it gets—"

"You mean like keeping it clean?" she asked.

Protests came from around the table.

"I could help with that, yes," Gwyneira continued eagerly despite our objections. "I don't know that much about housework. But if you say the house is safe, then I've seen the servants work and I could—"

"We don't need a servant." I smiled at her, attempting to

take any sharpness from my words. But, gods, what was Niko thinking, suggesting a *princess* clean a magical house that hadn't needed so much as a feather duster in years? "The house is fine, and you're more than welcome to stay as our guest. You don't need to—"

"You all saved my life. The least I can do is contribute in the home of those who helped me."

The previous hesitancy in her tone was gone, and determination now lined her words. There was fire under that politeness, and gods, if that wasn't strangely exhilarating to hear.

Just when I thought I couldn't be any more drawn to her than I already was...

And besides, how could I say no to that?

"Okay." I nodded, unable to take my eyes from her. "The house usually tends to itself, but... I'm sure it wouldn't mind some help."

She smiled, the expression like a ray of sunlight, and all that was left for me to do was pick my melted heart up from the floor.

11

DEX

Even cotton in my ears wouldn't have kept the sounds in the kitchen from reaching me.

I pressed my fingertips to my temples, squeezing my eyes shut and ordering myself to stay focused. A few minutes prior, half a dozen Huntsmen had ridden through the open castle gates. I'd tracked them as far as the edge of the mountain range before losing them in the shifting patterns of magic in the foothills.

They were after someone, and I had the sneaking suspicion she was about thirty feet away, sitting between four of my friends in our kitchen.

Probably smiling. Laughing too, though it was hard to hear her over the sound of the guys.

Not that I was listening.

I adjusted a small dial on the gilded edge of the mirror and locked my attention on the castle again, trying to force my brain back into the familiar patterns of strategy and planning that normally felt as comfortable as well-fitting boots.

Except for right now.

I gritted my teeth, tracking the movements of soldiers on the wall. The other Huntsman's plan of giving the queen an animal's heart must not have worked. Which meant now we had a problem, and it wasn't the one my cock wanted to make me believe I was facing—namely how to get that gorgeous woman into my bed *now*.

How could we protect her against the queen?

I snarled, pushing away from the desk, though that didn't do a damn thing to help me, since it only left me even more aware of how empty it was in here. Even the lights seemed dimmer, like all of the cabin was focused on her too.

My eyes flicked to the wood walls. Had she deceived the cabin? I wouldn't have believed such a thing were possible, but what other explanation was there?

Unless she *wasn't* a threat.

The hell she wasn't. She was human, for fuck's sake, and royal to boot. I needed to protect us *from* her, not protect her from anything at all.

No matter how much she drew me to her, and the closer I came, the less and less I remembered why I should stay away.

I snarled a curse at myself, raking a hand over my hair hard enough to rip a few strands out. This was nonsense. Worse, it was dangerous. I'd trusted my gut throughout my entire life, only for it now to betray me. Every instinct I had went awry at the sight of her, and the strangest thoughts raced through my head, bringing to mind fairytales and a word that never should have occurred to me.

Treluria.

But fantasy stories told by romantics wouldn't make me set aside the cold, hard truth. We didn't get trelurias and happily-ever-afters, no matter what my gut roared at the sight of her. We were the dwarves. The outcasts. We had our survival here, and safety too, and that was damn well enough.

It'd always been enough.

And she was the princess of Aneira, a nation that had practically made genocide and murder its national pastime for two gods-damned decades. Chances were, no matter how young and innocent and desperate she seemed now, she'd be just like the rest of them when she found out what we were.

She'd want us dead. She would run pell-mell for the nearest human and beg them to strike us down, no matter what we'd done for her.

In the end, humans sided with humans, no matter how you tried to help them. I knew that better than anybody. After all, the soldiers of my regiment had tried to kill me. Didn't matter that I'd just saved their lives. Didn't matter that I'd served with them since before the war began. We'd come under attack, dozens of soldiers were cut down, and there'd been no way out. I'd long since started questioning the war, so I hadn't wanted to hurt the giants, but I also hadn't wanted myself or the soldiers I served with to die. I'd made a tough call, stopped my own kind, and used my magic to save our asses.

Giant magic, the type humans didn't possess. The closest to magic humans came was through those rare souls born as witches or sorcerers, and that kind of magic was cold and hard like the gemstones the Jeweled Coven prized as reservoirs for their power. But the power of my kind felt like the earth, like weather and nature, as myriad and complex as the planet itself. I knew even when I was using it that the humans would be able to tell the difference.

But I'd saved their lives anyway, hoping my fellow soldiers would be sensible. That they'd see past the madness of Erenlian versus Aneiran to the man who'd just kept them from dying.

They'd tried to execute me as a spy for my trouble.

My gut churned as I forced myself back to focusing on the mirror, every laugh coming from the other room like a blade in my gut. Even since we'd seen it yesterday, the castle had changed. The black cloths on the windows and walls were gone now, far sooner than the end of any traditional mourning period. That the servants and courtiers hadn't objected to that was... odd. It went far beyond a faux pas and straight into disrespect for the fallen king. Yet I'd caught a glimpse of rolls of cloth being carried in through the gates, even as the Huntsmen rode away. From the colors, they looked like coronation fabric.

The queen was bold, but even the most arrogant ruler would likely have put up a pretense of care for the deceased.

Unless she'd used magic on them all, enchanting the court not to give a shit.

I exhaled. In our first few years here in the mountains, we'd heard tales about the queen, each more ludicrous than the last. Most had been whispered in taverns, shared between drunks too foolish to keep their mouths shut. Not long after, though, new stories started up. The taletellers were going missing in the night. Their bodies—if they were found—were torn apart as if by wild animals.

We'd assumed the king's guard were making examples of the rumormongers for spreading lies about his queen. The Witch War had given rise to all kinds of tales, but I knew survival required believing what was *possible*, not what was sensational. We'd still taken care to avoid the taverns for a long while after that, just in case any *other* stories spread—namely ones about seven large men who'd disappeared into the mountains after drinking their fill.

But now I wondered how many of those stories about the queen had been true.

Scowling, I adjusted the magic mirror again, turning my attention to the foothills and scanning as best I could for any trace of those Huntsmen. Whether the queen had remained in the castle or was out hunting the princess in all of this, I couldn't be sure. Truth be told, we almost never saw her, except at night.

And the gods knew there used to be plenty of stories about why, ranging from the foolish to the purely outrageous.

More laughter came from the kitchen, and this time, the princess's voice was easy to hear. The light sound of her amusement ran down my spine like an electrical current straight to my cock, bringing unbidden fantasies flashing through my mind, tormenting me with questions of what *other* sounds she might make.

I growled at myself. Gods, she wasn't ours. *Definitely* wasn't mine. She was easily a decade and a half younger than me, maybe more, and even if by some miracle she *didn't* try to kill us all the moment she knew what we were, she'd still never be interested in a common soldier like me.

She'd never understand what it meant to me, this irrational, core-deep groan that pled with me to go to her because she was mine to cherish, to protect, to fuck until she was limp with pleasure, satisfied and yet begging for more.

"Dammit, enough," I muttered to myself. "Fucking *enough,* you fool."

I gripped the edge of the table, ordering myself to stay put and not give in to the pull to go be near her. *With* her.

Anything.

"Hey, Dex," Clay called from the kitchen. "Come here a sec?"

Damn me if I didn't get up anyway, hurrying to be near the woman who was certain to destroy us all.

12

GWYNEIRA

After dinner concluded, there'd been some debate regarding where I would sleep, considering I was to stay with them, and the traitorous voice in my mind wanted to make an entirely inappropriate suggestion.

With them.

In their beds.

To resist the urge to volunteer that possibility, I'd barely said a word the whole time they debated. I was certain they thought me quite proper, perhaps even fragile. And truly, my classes in politics and etiquette were like a cloak around me now, stilling my tongue and keeping me from blurting out anything humiliating. But I couldn't hide from my own thoughts, utterly ludicrous though they might be.

I wanted each of them. They were as different from one another as the sun was from the depths of the earth, and yet I was drawn to them all. My body didn't want to pick. No, instead, my mind was flooded with delusions of having each of them, as if that were even a possibility.

Or rational. Or sane. Or what I even needed to be doing

right now, when my father was dead and my stepmother had taken the throne and everything in my world had ended in the space of only a day.

My chest ached, as if my heart was nothing but a ball of agony lodged behind my rib cage.

Sitting at the dinner table, I closed my eyes briefly to shove down the pain, hoping the men wouldn't notice as they debated. The sheer volume of what I'd lost felt like a mountain unto itself, poised on the brink of an avalanche. And I couldn't let it fall. The weight would crush me, and I'd never survive. So I focused here, on these men, on the remains of dinner and the beautiful little bouquet I hadn't had the heart to turn down, and I tried not to let my body's madness drive me to do something that would push these people away too.

Because the gods knew I couldn't have them all. No man would ever agree to such a thing. Few would even have agreed to the level of freedom Father had given me—training in government, history, and even brief lessons in weaponry before Melisandre had protested the idea of me learning to handle a sword. But the idea of all these men agreeing to be with me in that way?

Unthinkable.

And only proof of how mad I'd become to even imagine such a thing.

"So that settles it," Clay said, bringing my thoughts up short. "We expand the closet at the end of the hall."

I blinked, definitely having missed several turns of the conversation. "I-I'm sorry, did you say 'closet'?"

"Don't worry, Princess," Niko assured me, a smile on his face that made me want to trust him, no matter my trepidation. He truly was only a couple years older than me, but unlike any of the young men at my father's castle, he wasn't brash or boastful. Instead, there was something so calming about him, and I couldn't help but let my tension go in his soothing presence. "We'll make it nice for you. Much bigger than it sounds."

"And it's very defensible," Byron added, a note of practicality in his voice that I doubted ever truly left. He seemed analytical to his core, but in a way that was never cold or lacking compassion. No, he clearly devoted every bit of his intellect to the protection and care of those around him—and now, for reasons that were as kind as they were unfathomable, he'd decided to include me in that number. "There's no chance your stepmother or any of her Huntsmen will get near you without us noticing."

My mouth moved, a new kind of ache rising in me as I stared around at them. Even Dex had returned to join in the debate, and though he wasn't meeting my eyes, he appeared as resolute as the rest regarding what Byron had said.

It hurt, and it made no sense. These strangers thought so much of protecting me, while everyone else I'd known had turned their backs on me at a word from my stepmother.

Tears threatened to fall and I smothered them, forcing a smile onto my face instead. "Thank you."

Everyone but Dex beamed. My heart ached worse.

The twins, Byron, and Niko all rose to their feet, leading the way out of the kitchen while Dex stepped aside to make way.

"Is this okay with you?" I murmured to Dex as we climbed the steps behind the others.

He didn't look at me. "Of course."

I ran out of anything to say.

As a group, the men escorted me down the hall, pausing finally at a closed door at the very end.

"Would you like to do the honors?" Byron asked Dex.

For a moment, Dex regarded them all, something unreadable in his eyes. But he walked forward all the same and placed his hands on either side of the doorframe.

A chill swept my skin, though it didn't feel like the air had become any colder. More like something odd was passing around me, through me, like a gust of wind that left no trace of its passage. And even if nothing about the closed door changed, I would have sworn I could feel the room beyond shifting and expanding.

Breathless, I took a step backward, and I blushed when I noted several of the men glancing at me questioningly for the motion.

Dex lowered his hands, not even looking winded by the display of power. Stepping into the space he'd left, Clay and Niko each took a side of the door. "It's safe, Princess," Niko said with a sweet smile. "Promise."

I managed a weak smile in return, though it could barely get past the trepidation fluttering inside me.

The chill came again, but different. Cool like a rushing river on one side, somehow earthen on the other. The sensations rose in a wave and then faded, and I couldn't tell this time what had changed.

Turning the handle, Clay pushed open the door.

I swallowed dryly. The room beyond was easily as large as the one in which I'd woken up hours ago, and whatever had been in there before, now a large bed covered in a white blanket stood to the right while a chest of drawers waited against the left wall. A thick rug woven in rich reds and purples and pinks lay on the wooden floor, reminding me of spring. There was even a bouquet of flowers on the table beneath the window on the far side of the room.

"Do you like it?" Niko asked, a touch nervously.

I turned back, dumbstruck. They'd done that in moments. They'd done it with barely any effort at all.

"You're safe, Princess," Byron assured me. "None of this will harm you."

I wetted my lips, finding my words again. And despite my trepidation, I couldn't lie. "It's beautiful."

Even Dex smiled.

"We should let you get rest," Dex said, and I could hear the dismissal for the men in his tone.

Apparently I wasn't the only one.

"Goodnight, Princess," Lars said, his blue eyes warm despite their pale color, like a summer sky beneath which nothing could ever go wrong. "I'll have a nice breakfast for you in the morning. You like eggs?"

I nodded and he grinned.

One after the other, they each wished me goodnight, until at last only Dex remained.

"Thank you for your hospitality," I said.

He gave a small nod. "The guys will likely want to stay here tomorrow. Help you settle in. But ordinarily, we tend to leave fairly early, so if you wake up and we're gone, don't worry. Just ask the house for what you need, and it'll be there."

I glanced at the walls, anxiety rising in me again like a trapped bird. The men were one thing. Maybe, anyway. But I still didn't know how to feel about the fact I was literally surrounded by magic, inside a house that possessed its own opinions.

Dex stepped away from the wall, coming toward me. "Princess, I promise you. It's safe here."

I nodded, trying to believe what they'd all been telling me for hours—or at least to *look* like I did. I didn't mean to be rude. Neither they nor their home had shown signs of trying to harm me since they decided to let me stay.

But my stepmother had been trustworthy too, right up until the moment she betrayed me and Father both.

A tremble rolled through me, grief at his death feeling like a nightmare from which I surely would wake. But I never did, and the pain of it chewed at my insides like a dog. I closed my eyes for a moment, breathing shallowly, trying to get it under control.

"Hey." Warm hands took mine, making my eyes pop back open. Dex's customary seriousness was replaced by concern. "What is it?"

I started to shake my head. "Nothing. Thank you for—"

"Princess."

I looked away, my thoughts scattered by the warmth of his hands and the solidity of them holding me. "You... You're all just so kind."

He gave a small chuckle. "We could be assholes if it'd help? Hurr, hurr, woman. Where's dinner?"

A laugh burst from me, and he smiled. I found myself smiling too.

But the expression felt wrong when my father was lying dead in a crypt, somewhere I'd never even be able to visit for fear of being killed too.

Tears stung my eyes and I turned my face away. Exhaustion dragged at me, as if it was finally catching up after all the food and warmth of the evening, and it brought with it all the horrors that had come before. Even with every delicious dish that I'd eaten, I still felt hungry, as if a great hole had opened inside me and none of the food Lars had crafted could fill it. Likewise, the warmth of the house couldn't beat back the core of ice that seemed to have lodged in my middle.

Perhaps everything Melisandre had taken from me had doomed me to cold and hunger, no matter the kindnesses offered to me.

Dex's hand rose, one rough finger brushing my cheek and taking my tears with it. "Oh, gods, Princess. Please don't cry."

Grief and pain gripped me tighter at his kindness, and involuntarily, I moved closer, drawn by him and the gentle concern in his voice. His warmth was like a comforting blanket on a cold night, like a campfire driving back the dark. He felt so steady, like the world of chaos could rage around him and he'd survive it all.

I wanted to lose myself in that. In him.

I slipped a hand from his, taking his side, and beneath his sweater, I felt his chest catch. I risked a careful look up at him, afraid of what I might see. I was being too forward. Too reckless in this house of men I wanted so badly, who'd shown no sign of likewise wanting me.

But hunger and heat filled his eyes, sending a thrill straight through me to the flesh between my legs.

"Please?" I whispered, not even sure what I was begging for. Everything, maybe.

His hand turned, cupping my cheek, and my lips parted as desperate need rose in me like a flood. I stepped closer, the very air seeming to warm as I drew near him.

But resistance flashed across his face. "I... I should go." His voice was tense.

A shaky breath left me. His words were reason. Sanity and sense. But when he started to turn away, my grip tightened all the same.

"Please."

He looked back, and I couldn't find my voice. Of their own accord, my feet carried me even closer to him. He towered over me, and my other hand reached up to rest on his chest as if I could draw on the strength I felt there.

Air pressed from him beneath my palm. "You..." His eyes closed briefly, struggle clear on his face. "You've been through a lot today, Princess."

I didn't want to be reminded of that. I didn't want anything except to stop craving, stop aching.

And just feel.

I took his hand, drawing it to my lips and brushing kisses across the backs of his fingers. The tip of my tongue slipped out on impulse, tasting his skin.

He groaned and pulled his hand from mine, but only to draw me toward him. He bent, his lips claiming mine with something almost desperate in his intensity, while all the cold in me finally, *finally* washed away.

My heart beat harder as his hands slid around me, one on my back and the other raking up through my hair to hold me to him. His kiss was like fire and life itself, exhilarating and flooding my mind with light, and as his tongue plundered my mouth, I clutched him tighter, hungry for more. I'd never even kissed someone, but he didn't seem to care about my lack of skill. He moved us back until my calves hit the edge of the bed, and desire overrode everything else in my mind. My body ached for him. For this. For a way to forget everything that had come before and lose myself in something that felt like I'd needed it all my life, even if I'd only just begun to dream of it now.

Gripping his side, I started to sink down toward the bed.

His lips broke from mine. "Princess." His voice was ragged and he cleared his throat. "I don't want to take advantage—"

I reached behind my back, yanking with one hand at the laces on the vest and drawing in air with relief when they seemed to undo themselves. Never taking my eyes from him, I pulled the blouse down around my middle, exposing my breasts to him. I was half crazed, my mind lost in lust and need, and I barely recognized myself in the desperation. It was as if something wild had hold of me.

But I didn't care. I needed him. Needed all of them. My body was frantic with hunger to have him in me.

A breathless sound left Dex, and behind his back, the door swung shut of its own accord. "Have you ever been with a man before, Princess?"

My head shook, my eyes never leaving him.

The fire flared hotter in his gaze. "And you wish me to...?"

I pushed my breasts toward him, offering myself, and the words came to me from countless books I'd snuck from deep within the castle library. "Fuck me, sir. Please."

His nostrils flared, but the rest of him froze like a statue. Had I shocked him? Surely, I had. My silly fantasies were culled from books no one would have *dared* let me read if they'd known I'd found them buried deep in the library. Such words were certainly never meant to be spoken in real life.

Embarrassment searing me, I opened my mouth to apologize, but suddenly, Dex was moving again. In a smooth motion, he stripped off his sweater and the shirt beneath, exposing a chest of pure muscle lined by erratic scars like knife cuts I'd seen on soldiers at the castle. Tossing the clothes aside, he came toward me.

I couldn't breathe. Was he truly going to do as I asked?

With an intense focus, he cupped my breasts in his palms. His skin was rough, but the friction was deliriously pleasant. My mouth fell open with a silent cry as he pinched my nipples between his fingertips, and my legs parted of their own accord.

"Such a responsive little virgin," he murmured, and even if his words made a blush rise in my cheeks, something inside me preened at the approval in his voice, thrilled at pleasing him. "Are you wet for me already, little one?"

His eyes flicked to mine, almost as if checking my reaction. But the throbbing and moisture between my legs only grew at his words, and I nodded breathlessly.

"Good girl."

His hands left my breasts, descending to my breeches and unfastening the ties there too. Hurriedly, I reached up to his own breeches.

He tensed, a warning sound escaping him, and I froze.

"Hands down," he ordered, a tightness coming back to his voice.

I dropped my hands to my sides.

A small degree of tension leaked from him. He needed this control, I realized. I didn't know why, but it didn't matter. I'd give it to him, and when a hint of a pleased smile tugged at his lip, my body flushed hot at the sight.

Quickly, he stripped away his pants, leaving himself bare to me.

I exhaled shakily. He was magnificent. My tongue played

across my lips at the sight of his cock, upright and ready, thick as my wrist. I had no idea how someone so huge would fit inside me, but moisture soaked me at the desire to try.

I hesitated, torn between the desire to lie back for him right now and let him take me however he wished, and the need to taste him.

Uncertain, I leaned toward him. I wanted this in me. Needed it now. But first...

He made another gruff sound. My eyes snapped up to his. "Please, sir? Just a taste?"

Satisfaction filled his gaze. He gave a tight nod.

My heart pounding, I leaned forward again and teased my tongue around the head of his cock, tasting salt and spice and him. A groan left him, and I froze for fear I'd done something wrong, but when I looked up, his face was tense with desire.

His eyes dropped to mine, something so hungry and possessive in that gaze that a whole new thrill shot through me. I didn't *just* want him inside me. Suddenly, I wanted him to claim me so thoroughly, it would be as if he had scorched his lust into my flesh and bones, making me wholly his. My body throbbed with the desire for it. For him to do whatever he wanted, if only to bring a release to this need growing within me.

"You want me to fuck your mouth, little princess?" he murmured.

I gave a tiny nod.

His lips curled. "I will. But tonight I'm going to taste that virgin pussy of yours."

With movements so swift they stole my breath, he had

me on my back and yanked my breeches and blouse away, exposing me to him completely.

Running his gaze over me, he paused for only a moment, a question in his eyes.

"Please, sir," I whispered, spreading my legs for him. "Please."

The heat in his eyes grew. He ran a finger along my wet slit, teasing around my sensitive nub, and of their own accord, my hips jerked toward him, pleasure rioting from just that light touch. A smile pulled at the corner of his mouth.

"So sensitive."

Still smiling darkly, he dropped to his knees at the edge of the bed. Curiosity fluttered through me as he lifted one of my legs, placing it over his shoulder. Was he really...?

He bent closer. His tongue slid up my slit.

I gasped, my head falling back against the soft bed. Oh, gods, yes, he was.

A pleased sound left him, as if he liked what he tasted, and an instant later, he returned, sucking and licking between the folds of my flesh with dizzying talent. As his mouth kept up its ministrations, his fingers slipped into my entrance, crooking against my insides, unleashing pleasure all their own.

My fists clenched on the white quilt beneath me, gripping the fabric as I bit my lip to keep from moaning too loudly.

This was better than any fantasy.

I closed my eyes as he licked me in beautiful rhythm, as if he could read every twitch of my body. My nipples tightened and my muscles did as well, pleasure building hotter and higher inside me like a magic all its own.

One of his hands slid up my body to massage my breast, and my muffled moans became more frantic. Everything came down to his motions, his incredible mouth and hands. How had I never known this could feel this amazing? This *overwhelming*? Begging noises left me as I fought to stay still for him, my entire body tensed in desperate need to keep this going, make this never, ever—

Pleasure erupted through me in a blinding rush, stealing the room and the bed, flooding through my limbs and mind. I felt like pure light, bright and glittering, and as the room slowly returned to me, the afterglow of the orgasm left me with only peace, like slowly falling snow, in its wake.

As I sagged back onto the quilt, my eyes found him. He was watching me, and when I met his gaze, his lips curled into a pleased expression. "That's my good girl."

Desire surged in me again at his words. I spread my legs again and arched my back, my breasts rising toward him. "Please, sir. More."

He grinned.

13

DEX

I'd lost my mind, and I didn't give a shit.

Watching this woman come was the best thing I'd ever seen.

"I want you nice and relaxed, Princess," I said, taking up her leg again and moving into position to lick her again. I was telling the truth; she was a virgin, and gods, how I wanted her first time to be good for her. But her taste was also ambrosia, and I couldn't get enough.

Whatever she would have said was lost in another gasp as I teased her with my tongue. I smiled, and when I slipped my finger into her, she arched responsively to the motion, her beautiful coal-black hair falling around her in a wave and her pale cheeks flushed with pink like a delicate rose.

My cock ached, demanding to feel her wrapped around me, but I made myself concentrate as she came apart again and again. Whatever god had sent this woman to us, I owed them tremendously. And tomorrow, I'd talk to the others. Explain as best I could why I couldn't keep my distance, couldn't slow down, despite everything I'd said and believed.

Right now, I might as well have tried to resist the sunrise as fight this.

"Please," she begged breathlessly. "Gods, please, sir."

She sounded delirious with pleasure, and when she called me "sir"—a *princess*, for the gods' sakes, calling me that—it made my cock ache to fill her.

With a needy whimper, she tilted her hips toward me.

Desire surged higher in me, pulsing with a need to claim her that felt written on my bones. I craved filling her with my seed and letting the others fill her too, and I'd keep her with us forever, if only she'd agree, every inch of her body kissed and touched and fucked by each of us until we were engraved on her soul.

This was all madness, but damn if it wasn't worth it.

I moved over the top of her as she shifted higher on the bed, resting her head against the pillows. Never taking my eyes from hers, I pushed her legs farther apart and angled my cock until it brushed her wet entrance.

Her dark eyes widened, desire so strong in them I could drown.

"You want this?" I murmured.

An inarticulate pleading sound was her only response.

"Spread wider, then," I ordered.

She moved her legs farther apart immediately, and satisfaction pounded through me at how quickly she obeyed what I asked. Gods, it *was* like we were made for each other. Rocking forward, I eased carefully into her, stretching her opening, and she moaned.

"That's it. You'll take it all like a good girl, won't you, Princess? Every inch."

She nodded fervently and I felt her cunt twitch around me, turned on by what I said.

A thrill went through me. She wanted this as much as I did, and I couldn't resist that. Gods help me, she'd be mine, body and soul.

I pulled out and she made a pleading sound, but I didn't let her rest for long. Easing in deeper, I watched her face for any sign of pain or discomfort.

She looked euphoric.

I slipped a hand between us, massaging her clit as I began gently thrusting, desperate to take her but never wanting to cause her pain. She'd crave this again and again, if I had my way. I'd fuck her mouth, her ass, and make her come so many times she passed out from the pleasure.

"You're my good little princess, aren't you?" I murmured as she gasped beneath me. "You'll give me that wet, dripping cunt as much as I want."

She nodded, her eyes squeezed shut. "Yes, sir. Yes. Oh, gods."

I pushed myself into her deeper and she rocked against the bed. "You're mine to fuck, aren't you, Princess?"

She nodded again frantically.

"Say it."

"Yes, sir. I'm yours to fuck. I'm yours to—"

I thrust harder and she cut off with a moaning cry. I found her rose-red lips, kissing her and capturing her ragged pleas for more. Her hands gripped my sides, and her back arched beneath me, pushing her soft, luscious breasts against me as I drove her closer and closer to the edge.

I owed the gods so damn much...

A cry escaped her as the muscles inside her clenched down, gripping my cock in rhythmic spasms to wring out everything from within me. And I couldn't hold off any longer. Instinct took over as the orgasm claimed me, making me pump out all I had into her willing pussy.

Heaven. This was pure heaven.

As the orgasm faded, I sagged against the bed, careful to avoid crushing her. My cock settled inside her, still twitching out its last as I looked down at her.

She smiled up at me. "Thank you, sir."

My heart swelled. I bent again, kissing her briefly, and a smile tugged at my lips when I pulled away again. "Anytime."

She chuckled, but her smile faded as she glanced toward the door. Concern made me pause. Was she worried about the house? The magic?

"Do you think the others, um…" She hesitated. "Will they be upset you, um…"

Oh.

I searched for words to explain in a way that wouldn't result in her Aneiran sensibilities making her panic.

"No," I said. "They, uh…" I slid from within her and moved to the side to give her space. I didn't want her to feel trapped. "They won't."

She nodded, but her smile seemed sad.

"What is it?"

She hesitated. Climbing to her feet, she walked carefully across the room, candlelight playing over her naked skin. As if realizing what she'd done, she paused for a moment and then bent down to retrieve her blouse from the floor.

"Princess?" I prompted, though my eyes lingered on the beautiful curve of her ass. Gods, if I could grab those hips and plunge into her from behind…

"It's nothing," she said, drawing the blouse over her

head. The white fabric draped down past her hips, teas-ing me.

I pulled my gaze back up to her eyes. "You can tell me, Princess."

"I don't want to cause problems."

Now I was confused. "Problems?"

"You're all just... very attractive and..."

My brow drew down. Wait, what was she saying?

"I mean"—she shook her head as if dispelling a thought—"I'm glad you share my attraction to you. I hope the others don't— That is to say, I..."

She trailed off like she couldn't find the right words.

"Princess?" I stared at her, not sure I wasn't reading too much into things. I could be. But—

"I'm sorry." She shook her head. "I'm ruining this."

Oh, hell. "Are you attracted to more of us?"

Her eyes flicked toward me, the fear in them not disguising what I'd swear was a confirmation.

"I'm sorry," she said again. "I surely have offended you, and I—"

An incredulous scoff burst from me. Forget owing the gods. There wasn't thanks enough in the world for this. "*Offended* me?"

Wariness flickered over her face and it caught me. I couldn't blurt this out and risk terrifying her.

"Are you familiar with the practices of..." Gods, if I said giants, she'd panic. But was I being an asshole not to tell her the truth?

Maybe. Probably.

Yes.

Definitely yes.

"Gentresqua," I said instead as guilt began to chew

through everything we'd done. What had I been thinking, having her like that and not telling her who I was? Who *we* were?

Damn me, I hadn't been thinking. I'd tried to resist, but I'd been overcome. Whether there was a damn bit of truth to treluria or whether I'd just been thinking with my cock, it didn't matter. I should have kept more control of myself.

"Gentresqua?" she repeated. For a moment, she looked confused and then understanding flickered through her eyes. Her brow drew down. "You mean…" Her eyes went to the door, blinking, before returning to me with a trace of hope. "All of you… like some of their people…" She cleared her throat delicately, the propriety I suspected was her royal training vying with hints of the deliciously sexy minx I'd caught sight of beneath it all.

Her lips parted, her gaze skirting to the door again.

Holy fuck, she looked turned on by the idea, and even my guilt couldn't diminish how much I wanted to shout for joy at the sight.

"We're… we're not from there," I made myself say. "But… yes. We share." Sanity, showing up so late it wasn't even amusing, reared its head. Even if I thought she looked turned on, it'd still be good to check. "Does that bother you?"

A breathless sound left her as she looked back, her eyes darting past me to skip across the bed where we'd lain only a short while ago. "I must be mad," she whispered.

I hesitated, not sure what to make of that. Was she concerned about magic again? Did she think we'd placed a spell on her?

She looked up at me. "So if I… I mean…" She chuckled

like she couldn't believe herself. "If I was amenable to that too, would they…" She nodded toward the bed.

I kept myself from laughing, if only to stop her from thinking I was mocking her. "I'm fairly certain several of them would join us right now."

Her eyes widened, and she didn't seem to know where to look. "I… I'm rather tired." In the candlelight, I could see traces of a blush burning its way up her cheeks. "It's been a long day, and you're quite, um, *skilled*."

I cleared my throat at the pride that swelled in my chest. "Tomorrow, then, yes? To talk, at least." I paused, and I couldn't stop my smile. "Unless, of course, you want anything more?"

Her blush deepened. "That would be… Yes, talking, and…" She looked overwhelmed.

I took her hand and she smiled again. But when I gave the door a quick glance, she tensed and began extracting her fingers from mine.

"You need to go," she said. "Of course."

"Only if you want me to."

A trace of her smile returned. She still looked shy, and resolution settled inside me that somehow, I'd find a way to bring out that other side, the one she kept hidden, that had begged me to fuck her only a short while ago.

The gods knew she shouldn't need to hide who she was.

Discomfort moved through me as she shifted around, pushing the blankets aside and climbing into the bed, her brows rising in invitation for me to do the same. What did my own thoughts say of me? Of us, assuming the others didn't kick my ass for all of this?

And rightly so. We were all hiding who we were from

her, no matter how much magic we'd revealed. But what I'd just done?

I managed a smile as I joined her, and she nestled in close when I put my arm around her, one of her legs wrapping my own and bringing her delicious pussy close to me again. I was a dog for sleeping with her without letting her make a fully informed choice. But rejecting her now? That would hurt her too.

I closed my eyes, cursing to myself. Had the gods helped me or damned me? Or could I even blame them when it was my own doing that caused this?

I just hoped they'd give me a way to resolve this that didn't drive her away.

And that I hadn't ruined everything before it'd even had a chance to begin.

14

GWYNEIRA

When I opened my eyes, Dex was gone.

Blinking in the bright morning light, I looked around the empty room. A thick blanket lay atop the quilt, as if he'd placed it across me before leaving, and a stack of new clothes sat on the dresser, complete with a new pair of boots on the floor. But the door was shut again, and no other sign of him was in the room.

I bit my lip, not sure what to make of last night. The space between my legs ached from what we'd done, a delicious sort of pain that asked for more—and soon. My body burned with the memory of his hands on me, his words in my ears, and I blushed to think of the things that had come from my own mouth in response.

Except... he'd seemed to enjoy them.

The gods knew I had.

I studied the door, which had so thoughtfully closed itself for us last night. I still couldn't quite wrap my mind around what he'd told me. That, like the rumors of some people in Gentresqua, this man and his companions also shared when it came to partners. The thought was surely too good to be true.

And as for how much I wanted that?

I dropped my gaze from the door, pressing a hand to the bed where he'd done such amazing things with me. Was I simply hiding behind the fear of madness? Or was I insane already? Either way, I had to admit the truth.

I wanted them, and if they truly welcomed that, then there was no reason to continue telling myself I was wrong to crave such a thing. My life was already in shambles. Finding some pleasure here might be all that was left for me.

Pushing aside the blankets, I swung my legs over the edge of the bed, only to wince as my hips and lower regions protested the motion with remnants of aching from last night. Breathing steadily for a moment, I waited for the throbbing to fade and then rose more carefully to my feet. Despite the wintry chill that coated the window in a beautiful pattern of frost, I only felt slightly cold as I crossed the room to the dresser and retrieved the clothes and boots. While I pulled them on, I strained to hear anything from the rest of the house, but I couldn't detect signs that the men had woken yet.

Perhaps they'd left. Even though Lars had promised a breakfast, and Dex said they'd stay today, maybe something had drawn them away.

Trepidation fluttered in my middle. What if my stepmother had found us?

Breathing slowly to remain calm, I opened the door to the bedroom and peered into the hall. All along the corridor, the other bedroom doors were closed.

Maybe they were still asleep.

Pausing for a moment, I considered my options, but if

they still slumbered within, then waking them wouldn't be any way to start my first day here.

Better to go downstairs and see what I could do to start assisting with this place, not that it appeared to need any cleaning. Even the trim along the corridor walls was free of any trace of dust.

I crept down the hallway, the perfectly fitted boots not making a sound on my feet. As I reached the stairway at the opposite end of the hall, I paused, the low murmur of voices reaching me, and a chill stole over me.

I couldn't make out the words, but they didn't sound pleased.

Glancing back at the room, I debated waiting until they were done, but how was I to know when that would be?

And if my actions last night had caused problems after all, I should do what I could to help remedy the situation.

Carefully, I crept down the steps.

"—should have *told* her," Roan snapped.

"I know." Remorse filled Dex's voice.

An incredulous sound followed. "What do you think she's going to say when she finds out what we—"

Someone cleared their throat loudly, cutting Roan off, and a moment later, Niko appeared at the base of the stairs. His calm had transformed into an edginess that made it seem as if he worried the air itself might explode. In careful tones, he said, "Good morning, Princess."

Anxiety rose in me again. "Good morning."

Niko's eyes darted to the side, and Byron appeared next to him. No matter how articulate he'd been at dinner last night, now the copper-haired man appeared to search for words before finally settling on simply saying, "Perhaps you should join us in the study?"

I nodded, watching them both as I descended the steps. This wasn't how I'd imagined speaking with the others would go last night. Moreover, what had Roan meant, if I found out?

"Is everything okay?" I asked.

Byron hesitated again. "Please." He gestured for me to go on.

My heart started to pound. Walking past him, I continued toward the study, not sure what I'd find within.

Dex stood on the far side of the room, half turned to a window. All the others were there too, even Ozias, who'd never made an appearance at dinner last night.

But none of them looked pleased. Far from it. Dex wouldn't even meet my eyes. Roan appeared furious, as did Clay, while Byron and Lars seemed concerned, and Ozias' expression was so grim I wondered if he meant to kill me.

"What's going on?" My hands gripped one another, my knuckles turning white. What would I do if they cast me out now? Where would I go? "If I have offended you in some way, I truly—"

"It's not that," Byron reassured me quickly.

I stepped aside as he moved past me into the study. "What is it, then?"

"It's that I shouldn't have—" Dex cut off, grimacing. "That is, I should have talked to you before..." He twitched his head to the side as if to indicate what we'd done.

"Talked to me about what?"

"Who we are."

My brow drew down. "What's that mean?"

Dex looked away. Around the room, the others shared a glance, almost as if trying to see who would be the one to answer me.

At last, Byron sighed. Folding his hands like a teacher bracing himself for giving a student bad news, he said, "Our people are the giants, Princess."

I blinked. Blinked again. And the words still made no sense. "W-what?" My gaze skipped across all of them. "That's not—"

"But," Byron continued in the same even tone. "Our people call *us* dwarves."

I shook my head, whether to deny the word or the rest of it, I didn't know. Giants or dwarves, the men didn't look a thing like the Erenlians I'd seen as a child. Those had been enormous monsters, their backs bowed, their hands the size of a grown man's torso and their faces haggard. And no matter how they appeared to suffer, my father reminded me those people had climbed the tower and crushed my mother, and they would have done the same to me.

"We don't mean you a bit of harm, Princess," Clay said. "I swear."

A strangled sound escaped me, and I took a step back, but it only brought me closer to Niko.

"You're safe, Princess." There was a note of pleading in his kind voice, as if begging me to believe him. "We would never hurt you. Our people would never have hurt your mother, either. Erenelle was peaceful, and we—"

I held up my hands as if to stop the mad words, retreating from him too. The open door to the study beckoned behind me, offering an escape. But would the house stop me? It hadn't yet. But if I tried to leave, would I become their prisoner?

They'd lied to me. Or lied through omission, which was just as bad, letting me trust them, even *like* them.

Gods, I'd had sex with... and they were...

"Princess," Dex started apologetically.

The word was like the crack of one blade against another, sending adrenaline spiking through me. And then I was moving. Fleeing the study and racing down the hall like a rabbit, no rational thought in the motion.

But it wasn't like rational thought was my forte. Not given my behavior last night.

My breaths were ragged and searing on my lungs. The walls of this magic house built by giants felt as if they were closing in on me, though I couldn't tell for certain if they moved. When I reached the front door, it flew open at my touch, not trying to trap me at all. With a frantic gasp, I tore out into the snowy clearing.

The door didn't shut behind me. No fence or wall rose to threaten me. But that changed nothing for the panic still gripping me hard. I didn't stop moving, racing for the forest and the mountain and anywhere besides here.

A line of stones passed beneath my boots, and the air felt like it tingled as it touched my face, but still I didn't stop. Not until the trees were between me and the cabin. Not until the path was long since gone. Rocks and undergrowth caught my feet, sending me stumbling. Branches swiped my face, and when at last I came to the edge of a river, I had to pause, if only because there was no way across.

Was it the giants' doing?

Rough breaths left me, shallow and desperate. Shaking hard, I sank down onto a boulder on the riverbank. My body ached all over, and chills so much deeper than the winter cold radiated up from inside me. Giants. I'd been in the company of giants. I'd even slept with one.

And gods help me, I'd craved them all.

How could I not have seen it? True, they weren't the size

of giants, but they were taller and broader than any other men I'd ever laid eyes on. And they worked in mines, for the gods' sakes. Yes, other people worked mines besides the giants. But still. How much more of a fool could I have been?

They could have killed me.

Shudders rolled through me. They could have. They really could have. But instead, they'd...

They'd...

I raked my hands into my hair and then clenched my fists on the strands, the sharp points of pain bringing me focus. My eyes locked on the frigid stream of water bubbling between rocks covered in ice and snow, as if the liquid might have an answer when nothing else did.

The men—the *giants*—had been kind to me. Even when they knew who I was, they still had been. Of anyone on earth, I should have been an instant target. Gods above, their people were locked in the mines for the sole purpose of protecting the world from their violence and cruelty, and yet those seven men—knowing I was the daughter of the king who'd imprisoned their people—hadn't lifted a hand against me.

Had it been some kind of game, all to toy with me?

To sleep with me?

Shudders radiated from my middle as if to shake me apart. Their people had crushed every bone in my mother's body. Giants from Erenelle had climbed the castle tower and murdered her only a few feet from my crib. And they would have killed me too. Only my stepmother's desperate intervention had spared me from being their next victim.

My fingers loosened on my hair.

Only... my stepmother...

Slowly, my hands dropped.

"Oh, gods," I whispered, icy horror spreading through me as if the river had risen enough to make me drown.

What had I believed? What had I always, *always* been told? That Melisandre saved me. That she stood alone against the giants, the only one between me and death when giants murdered my mother.

The very woman who'd accused me of killing my father, who'd set me up and probably murdered my poor maid as well…

I'd believed she was my savior.

Because that's what I'd always been told. What my father and *everyone* had been told.

By her.

"She lied." I trembled. "Oh, by the gods, she lied to us all."

I looked back, staring up at the forest and the mountain while fat flakes of snow drifted down. My whole life, I'd believed the giants to be monsters, but when I stood on the portico, cheering with all the rest as they were marched into the capital, destined for the mines, what had I *truly* seen?

Sadness. Pain. A people bent and struggling not to be broken. And for what? The word of a woman no one had even *met* before that night.

Gods, had she cast a spell on us? Done to my father and the guards what she did to Harran and the rest, making them her puppets, believing any story she wanted? Why else would my father have trusted her or married her only days after my mother died? Growing up, I'd only been told it was romantic, but…

We started a *war* at her word.

I exhaled, shaking all over. The Giant War… all those dead…

All those my own people killed...

Nausea twisted my core. I wished I could lay the blame at her feet wholesale, but I wasn't sure. Even if her lies started it, we'd all been so afraid, so convinced the Erenlians were monsters. Everyone I knew believed it. We spoke of them in whispers and watched for any who might be an Erenelle spy. That couldn't have *only* been her doing. I'd studied enough history to know how fear traveled, how it moved like a disease through a village, a city, a country. No matter how it started, fear could take on a life of its own, metamorphosing into something darker and uglier over time. And what we'd done in *response* to that fear...

Tears stung my eyes. Sweet gods, *we* were the monsters. We'd locked up an entire nation, an entire *species*, and we'd never once listened to their cries of innocence.

Because we'd only believed our own fear and her lies.

My eyes strayed along the mountainside. Seven men were up there somewhere, and they had every reason to hate me. But they'd chosen kindness instead.

And I'd repaid it with horror.

Unsteadily, I pushed to my feet while snow landed on my skin, barely even melting in the cold. I didn't know for certain in which direction the path to the cabin lay, but hopefully if I returned up the mountainside, I'd find it.

And the gods only knew what I could say to them when I did, assuming they even let me in the door again. "Sorry" was *laughably* not enough.

Hugging my arms to my middle for warmth, I started back up the path. The ground was slicker than I remembered from my panicked state, and I caught myself over and over as I made my way up the rough slope. How far had I run? How long had it been since I fled? From the featureless white sky above me, I couldn't tell the hour, but as I continued into the woods, it felt as if time had simply decided to stand still.

And as for where I was...

I stopped, turning in a circle and finding only never-ending trees in each direction. The snowfall had obscured my trail, and no one way was more promising than the next.

Shivers radiated from my core. I'd survived nearly freezing to death once, but only because of those men and their magical home. But without the cabin or the... dwarves? Giants? Whatever I should call them now?

Gods, I was in trouble.

I bundled my arms closer to my body. Maybe if I found a cave—

"Princess."

Gasping, I whirled. Ozias stood only a few yards away. I hadn't heard a single footstep to announce his approach.

I stared at him. Of them all, he'd always looked the wildest, with eyes that seemed to fix on me like those of a feral beast debating whether to go for my throat. But the massive weaponry on his back and his long, gnarled hair and beard made him seem more like a powerful warrior of old, one of the fighters I'd read about in myths who fought in ancient wars and then retreated from civilization to live in the wilds, never coming back because they were more at home in the woods than around any humans. That he'd killed before wasn't a question to me. No one had eyes like that without knowing how to take a life. Standing here now, with snow falling around us in the silence, I felt so small before him, a twig he could snap with a single blow. Yet the wildness in him called to me too, as if something in me craved that freedom, the rush of challenging a predator and discovering I was strong enough to survive.

But until this moment, I'd never been so near to him, and to look at him, I couldn't tell if his dislike of me had changed. For all I knew, he planned to kill me and only thought it best to give me warning before he struck.

"Why are you here?" I whispered.

"They asked me to find you."

I shifted my weight in the snow. "Why?"

"To bring you back safely."

"They want me to come back?"

His dark eyes narrowed with curiosity. "They didn't want you to leave."

"And you?"

In silence, he stared at me, and I quivered inside. Gods help me, I did want him. It was madness, same as ever. Foolishness too. I'd never lost my head over men or boys back home, and even in the face of someone I knew had to be a killer, I couldn't quite bring myself to run.

But I couldn't read the look that passed over his face, and without even moving a muscle, it felt as if he moved away from me, adding a distance between us as cold and barren as the winter that surrounded me.

Without a word, he turned and started back through the forest.

A shaky breath left me. That wasn't a yes, but then, it wasn't really a no either.

Regardless, the others were waiting, and I had something to say to them.

I only prayed they'd listen.

❄

We walked through the woods in near silence, with only my own missteps on branches and rocks making any sound. Ahead of me, Ozias passed through the forest like he was born of it. He never said a word to me, and by the time we reached the clearing, I was a ball of nerves from worry that the others would be equally closemouthed.

But I'd still talk to them, even if they didn't respond.

The air tingled slightly as I passed the line of stones at the edge of the clearing, and I shivered. That had to be the magic defense they'd told me about. The one I shouldn't have been able to get past. That I could now either meant nothing or was a good sign they wanted me to return.

I hoped it was the latter.

The door swung open before we reached it, though no one was there. Ozias paused and then grunted, some trace of irony in the sound. Without a word, he motioned for me to go ahead of him.

Swallowing nervously, I did as he asked.

The warmth of the cabin surrounded me when I walked inside, and from the study near the end of the hall, I could hear the low murmur of voices. Taking a steadying breath, I made myself continue on until I reached the door.

"—find her out there, it'll be Ozias."

"Yeah, but what if the queen—"

Clay cut off as Lars put a hand to his shoulder, and to a man, the others followed the twins' gazes to where I stood.

"Gwyneira." Dex came over to me quickly, snagging a blanket as he moved.

I wasn't sure what to say. It was the first time any of them had called me by my name rather than my title, but it didn't feel wrong to hear them use it.

It felt safe.

He seemed to catch himself as he came closer, though. Watching me like I might bolt again, he carefully wrapped the wool around me and then stepped back, and the military-like tension I'd seen on him when we first met closed around him as solidly as the blanket around my shoulders. "Come in?"

I nodded, giving him a nervous smile. "Thank you."

He nodded once, still eying me cautiously.

I stepped past him, turning my nervous expression on the others. They didn't look much different from Dex in their own ways, none of them making a single move as if concerned about what I might do. "I wanted to say something."

Clay's blue eyes darted to the others, every trace of his jovial nature subsumed beneath caution. "Okay. What?"

I drew a breath. "I... I'm sorry." A few of them shifted their weight warily, as if bracing for something. I pressed onward. "She lied, didn't she? My stepmother with her stories of..." I felt bad even repeating it. "Of giants climbing the tower and killing my mother. She lied."

Silence answered me for a long moment.

"Yes," Dex said quietly, still as rigid as a soldier.

A shudder rolled through me and I nodded. "I'm sorry. For believing it, for..." Gods, I felt sick, and the words hurt so much, but truth was the only way through this. I wouldn't hide behind lies. "For being glad your people were locked up. For cheering. For..." Tears stung my eyes. "For all of it. I'm so sorry. I didn't know. I believed her, and I acted horribly, and I know it's not enough to just say I'm sorry, but..." I squeezed my eyes shut, aching inside. "I'm so sorry."

The silence returned for a moment, and I couldn't even

bring myself to look at them. But then a soft rustle broke the stillness.

"Sit down?" Byron offered gently.

My eyelids cracked open in time to see him motion to a chair, his bright green gaze trained on me. My mouth moved, wordless. I didn't want to take one of their seats. But then, he was also offering it.

I crossed to the chair and sank down onto the edge of the leather. Drawing a shaky breath, I waited, but no one spoke.

"Who..." I swallowed, pushing the words out into the silence. "Who were the giants? Really? Please?"

A moment passed.

"Good people," Byron said quietly.

"Gentle," Niko added, a hint of his kind smile returning.

Dex scoffed. "Says you." Silence returned for a moment, and when he spoke again, the ice in his voice was gone, tinged by a regret that hurt to hear. "But nothing like the Aneirans said."

I closed my eyes.

"It's not your fault, Princess," Niko said quietly.

"How?" I looked up at him. "How is it not, when I benefited from it? I lived in a castle defended by weapons made of the ore they mined. I enjoyed comforts bought by trade of their unpaid labor. The economy of my entire *nation* was bolstered because we used your people. How is it not my fault too?"

"You didn't lock them up," Lars said.

"But I didn't let them go, either."

"Then," Byron said, calm logic in his even tone, "when you rule on that throne, you make it right."

I looked over at him. His face was somber, and somehow, it stabilized me. Not forgiving but not condemning, it simply... was.

And so was what I had to do.

A shaky breath entered my lungs, deeper than I felt like I'd breathed in a while. By now, it was certain my stepmother had taken the throne. Why wouldn't she? And the gods only knew what she'd do with it. But what she'd *already* done was clear. Murdered the king. Initiated a war that had killed, scattered, or locked away an entire nation of people. She'd set all of Erenelle up as her scapegoats, same as she'd done to me, and for too long, I'd done nothing but react and run in fear of all her lies.

But I was my father's daughter. I was the princess of Aneira. I was done with letting mindless fear drive me, and if I wanted anything to get better, then I was going to need to do more than stay alive. I had to take back my home.

Even if I had no idea how to do that.

I looked at the beautiful men—the beautiful *giants*—around me. I owed it to them, to my father, even to my poor maid Fironia, to try. So many people had been hurt or killed by my stepmother. Defeating a witch seemed impossible, but then, these men had already proven magic wasn't what I'd believed it was all my life.

Maybe I could even learn it myself.

A shiver rolled through me, all my old beliefs trying to rise up and argue that surely this was the very madness I'd been warned about.

Exhaling sharply, I pushed them aside. "I know I don't have any right to ask more of you than you've already done, but..." I braced myself against the way my insides still quivered at the words I was about to say. "Will you teach me magic? Help me learn to use it so I can stop her and set your people free?"

Surprise flickered across their faces as they glanced to one another, but slowly, Byron began to nod. "Yes, I will."

"If you agree that we also teach you to fight with weapons," Dex said, iron in his voice. "Not just magic."

"*Lots* of weapons," Lars added, his blue eyes wide.

Clay nodded at his twin brother's words. "Every damn one of them."

I nodded. In the space of a day, so many things I'd believed all my life had been proven a lie. And maybe I *was* mad. Maybe magic had made me take leave of my senses, just as Melisandre always said it would.

But maybe that was a lie too.

"Thank you," I told them. "All of you."

Dex's lip twitched. "See if you're still thanking me when training kicks your ass."

Tears and a laugh tangled together in my throat, coming out as a choked chuckle.

He extended a hand to me, pulling me up from the chair. "Let's get started."

I followed him out of the room. Ultimately, whether I was insane or not didn't matter. What happened to the giants was wrong, and the first chance I got—*every* chance I got—I was going to confront it. Even if I'd never be able to make up for everything that had been done, everything I'd participated in, I could still change it for the future. I could take back my throne and use that power to stop their suffering.

Somehow, I could make that much right.

15
MELISANDRE

Six weeks later

Weeks of spells to detect even a trace of her. Weeks of soldiers crawling over that damned mountain range to find her.

And nothing.

The blood-sniffing dogs couldn't find a scent. My vampire servants scoured the night and located nothing. The human soldiers were less than useless, and more than a few had slipped and fallen to their deaths on those slopes, if they hadn't just frozen entirely. The Huntsman continued on, a puppet on my string, but even he hadn't been able to tell the guards much beyond where he'd let the girl go. The day after she escaped, my spells had sent up a momentary flash from somewhere in the mountains, but the chaotic magic leaking from the Wild Lands instantly scattered it like light reflecting from inside a crystal. And then even that had vanished.

Not a trace of her had appeared since.

The slithering Voidborn churned in the mirror behind me. They were growing more and more restless—and hungrier too. I could hear them muttering and grumbling, their bloodlust unslaked.

I didn't turn, my eyes on the maps spread out on the table before me, so many mountains now marked by red slashes as location after location proved fruitless. The girl was either nowhere—which was impossible—or she'd died in a chasm so deep that she couldn't escape and the dogs couldn't find her.

Which would mean all my plans to turn her, to offer her up in my place, had failed.

The muttering grew louder. I closed my eyes, desperation pressing at me. All these years of planning...

I walked away from the table. My efforts wouldn't be for naught. I wouldn't *let* them be. Those creatures wouldn't feast on me, no matter what bargains I'd once struck with them. But I couldn't go out in the sunshine to search. Even my protections wouldn't hold endlessly. And if she'd died and risen already, she would be trapped by the sun entirely. I had my humans searching every cave and overhang, though I knew they couldn't understand why. So there shouldn't have been anywhere on those damned mountains she would be able to hide.

Unless...

I looked back toward the maps on the table. Nothing lived out there. Everyone knew that. The Witch War had swallowed whole nations and turned the farther reaches of those mountains into a wasteland.

Yet, what everyone knew was often wrong, and not every witch of the Jeweled Coven had been caught. I had the former queen herself to thank for that. And if those old crones were up there somewhere, hiding her, thinking to rob me of my prize...

I couldn't target them directly. Their magic would have seen to that. But I knew spells those cowardly fools wouldn't dream of touching, and I could bend and break nature itself, forcing it to serve me whether it wanted to or not.

Surely the trees and the wildlife knew where to find Gwyneira, and how to drive her from whatever hole those witches were currently hiding her inside.

Turning to the mirror, I lifted my hands toward it, calling upon the dark power I'd claimed years ago. Magic seethed beneath the reflective surface and shadowed shapes flashed past— slits of eyes, gaunt faces, more teeth than anything this side of the glass had ever owned.

And those monsters *loved* this plan.

I smiled. "Mirror, mirror, on the wall..."

16

GWYNEIRA

"Three gemstones here, a piece of spruce there, and concentrate..."

Nothing happened.

Again.

"Dammit!" I shoved away from the table, tears burning in my eyes. For weeks now, I'd been studying magic, pouring over every book and lesson Byron gave me. The magic of giants wasn't exactly the same as that of witches or sorcerers, though the scholar had studied enough about them all that he had no doubt he could still guide me in developing my own power.

That was, he *had*. And then weeks had gone by. And more weeks. And even the most basic of spells that I tried still failed.

No, not failed. They'd have had to react at *all* to fail.

I might as well have been trying to learn how to fly for how little I could do.

Scrubbing a hand over my eyes, I turned my back on the table and rose to my feet. Despite my struggles, I knew the men still believed I had magical ability buried inside. They seemed convinced of it. By now, Byron had spent more hours than I could count showing me spells and lending me his precious books of magic. When I floundered early on, he'd pivoted, the consummate teacher and every bit the scholar I heard he'd been training to be. He asked the others for help, and without question, the men had stepped up. Niko demonstrated over and over how to charm everything from flowers to seeds, while Clay and Lars did the same with water and fire and food and cloth. Even if our sources of power differed, they hoped some part of theirs would trigger an echo in me, giving me a sign of how to produce the same result in my own way.

But still, nothing happened.

For a time, I'd found an outlet for my frustration with weapons training. Dex lived up to his word, making me regret ever agreeing to learn more about physical fighting. He was relentless, polishing up every rusty skill I had from years before and insisting I learn countless more besides.

The man swore he'd never been anything more than a regular soldier, but gods, even the generals back home in the castle weren't as driven as him. And thus there'd been no option of pursuing anything physical with him or the others. Not when it was all I could do to crawl up the stairs each night, my every bone and muscle aching before I collapsed unconscious into bed.

But the men never wavered, determined that I'd make up a lifetime of magical and martial learning as fast as I could absorb the knowledge. Only Roan and Ozias stayed away, doing their work in the mines and then disappearing into their rooms once they returned home.

And I tried. The gods knew I tried. But when it came to

magic, none of the others' assistance changed a thing. As the weeks wore on, I started begging off Dex's trainings and avoiding the others too, pleading instead that they leave me be to study on my own up in my bedroom.

I'd been so grateful when they agreed, if only to escape the worry that I'd started to spot in their eyes.

And why shouldn't they be concerned? I'd promised to help them, and I couldn't master even the most basic of spells. Gods damn me, given every failure I'd had over the past several weeks, I was starting to suspect my gifts were reserved for *not* freezing to death on mountainsides and for crossing magical barriers without realizing I'd done it.

Not useless, but not particularly helpful in taking the throne back. Even if I did get past any magical defenses around the castle, the entirely *human* defenses would still see me coming.

And probably shoot me on the spot.

I sighed, reaching for the mug of tea on the dresser nearby.

The cup was cold. The contents had a thin layer of dust floating on them.

Damn, damn, damn. That happened *way* too frequently these days. I lost track of time and next thing I knew, it was morning or night or simply had been hours in which I hadn't eaten or slept—though it was hard to tell the hour regardless. I'd covered the window ages before, tired of the sunlight burning my eyes. My nerves were frayed, and my body seemed to have given up on me. I rested when I couldn't stay awake any longer. Ate when I remembered to be hungry. And when I did sleep, all I had were nightmares of my stepmother chasing me, laughing about how she'd find me or how I continued to fail. So this... this was what mattered.

For the giants. For the people currently suffering at my stepmother's hand—because the gods knew someone would be.

For my father.

A dull ache sawed at my insides when I thought of him, and I shoved it down as always. According to what Byron and Dex saw in the magic mirror, Melisandre had taken the throne a mere day after I escaped her, and only the gods knew what she was going to do with it. But somehow, I'd take it back. I'd find justice for my father and for the giants currently locked in the mines. Then... *then* I'd stop.

But not before.

I cast a half glance back at the table, but my fingers shook when I reached for the small branch of spruce. Cursing under my breath, I dropped my hand back to my side. In theory, the arrangement was a simple defensive spell using the raw gemstones as a way of channeling my magical energy and the twig as the thing I was supposed to protect. In reality, I'd been staring at that little collection for what felt like days—gods, it really *might* have been days—with absolutely nothing happening. Not a defensive barrier. Not a flicker of light. Hell, at this point I would have taken the whole twig going up in flames if only for the novelty of *something* happening from my efforts.

At this rate, the little branch was going to decay naturally before I learned magic—assuming I even could.

I raked a hand through my hair, finding tangles, and I scowled all over again. Tugging them out, I glared around the room. I would swear the walls were laughing at me. An entire house of magic, and I couldn't manage *this*.

Snagging the mug, I headed for the hall. I'd eat something. Remake my tea. And come back and make a damn defensive shield around that twig if it killed me.

Lanterns burned along the walls of the corridor when I left the room, meaning it was probably night or early morning. A chill clung to the air just as it always did, never seeming to fully warm the cabin no matter how high the flames in the fireplaces burned. The doors along the hall were closed, but when I reached the stairs, I could see more light coming from the first floor. Perhaps it was evening, then? Gods, I needed a clock.

Clay's voice carried from the kitchen, and from the sound of it, he was talking to his brother. The twins had a certain indefinable quality to their voices that only happened when they spoke solely to each other. I'd noticed it on the few occasions I'd stopped by the kitchen while the men were having food and my body's cries for sustenance had become too powerful to ignore. Those times were rare, though, and not just because I barely remembered to eat at an ordinary hour anymore.

I needed to fix this. Change this nightmare, for their sakes and mine. And until I did that, how could I focus on anything when every day that passed was one more in which their people were chained and my stepmother sat on my father's throne?

How could I relax at a dinner table when their people never could?

Hesitating, I glanced up the stairs. Coming back later would be easier. Less awkward, probably.

Clay's voice cut off. "Princess? That you?"

I grimaced, turning to retreat, but he leaned his head around the corner before I made it very far.

"Hey," he said.

I stopped. "Hello. I was just—"

"How about you come get some food, eh?" He left the kitchen and walked toward me as if to bring me back with him.

"I really should just—"

"Please?"

I faltered. Beneath his normally light tone, I thought I heard worry. Again.

And gods, it hurt.

"I'm fine, really."

"Maybe just take a break for a bit, then, yeah?"

Fidgeting with my sleeve, I glanced toward the kitchen again. Something smelled amazing in there, and my stomach began to gnaw at my insides in response. I wouldn't be able to focus if I returned upstairs, not now that my body had gotten the upper hand in reminding me I needed to eat.

"Yeah, okay."

I didn't miss the flicker of relief on his face, but he masked it quickly with a smile. Stepping aside, he motioned for me to precede him into the kitchen. I couldn't quite meet his eyes as I walked past.

In the kitchen, Lars set a plate of roast meat on the table and smiled at me. "Just in time."

I glanced around, but I didn't see anyone else. "Are the others coming?"

"Hmm?" Lars placed a jar of water on the table too. "Ah, no. They're asleep. It's just us."

My curiosity deepened. "Why are you still up?"

He glanced at his brother, something guarded flashing through his blue eyes. "Oh, we couldn't sleep, so we thought you might like the company if you came downstairs."

It felt like there was more to that statement, but my thoughts were muzzy and I couldn't track it. "And you were making that just for you two?" I nodded at the food.

He gave me a quizzical look. "For you."

I blinked and glanced back at Clay standing by the door. Magic. Of course. And he'd done it just like *that*.

Weeks of frustration burned in my chest, stabbing me like a hot iron poker, and I tried to cover it with a tight smile. "Apologies, but I should get back to—"

"You need to eat, Princess," Clay interrupted, stepping over to block the doorway as I started toward it. The seriousness on his jovial face looked out of place, and I couldn't hold his blue gaze for long.

"Torturing yourself won't change anything." Lars regarded me from beside the table, not coming closer.

I shook my head immediately. "I'm not—"

"When is the last time you ate?" he continued. "Or slept? Magic takes energy, and you're running yours into the ground."

"I'm really not—"

"Princess." Clay's hand touched my arm.

I flinched away, retreating from them both. "I need to fix this. I can't..." My frustration felt like a lead weight filling my chest, making it hard to take in air. "I have to stay focused. I'm sorry. I... I can't..."

"You will," Lars assured me, somehow sounding optimistic about my chances even when there was zero evidence to support it. "But how about some food first?"

"No, I'm sorry. There really isn't time."

His gentle smile was encouraging. "Sure, there is. Just for a few minutes, eh?"

My mouth moved, but I couldn't find an answer for him. My heart felt like it was pounding hard and yet far away, like I was starting to float free of my body, and I couldn't afford that. I needed to stay focused.

And meanwhile, they were both watching me, an intensity in their matching blue eyes like they were preparing to grab me if I bolted.

"Yeah, just a short break." Clay smiled. "What could that hurt?"

"No, I—"

"Come on, Princess. Just eat a little something."

"No, dammit! She'll get away with it!"

Both men went silent at my cry, and then Lars took a careful step forward. "What's that?"

My head shook as trembling radiated through me like I was freezing from the inside. "She's going to get away with it. If I can't fight her, then she..." The ground felt unsteady, but surely the house wouldn't be trying to knock me over. "She'll get away with killing my father and taking the throne and your *people...*"

I wavered on my feet and Clay's hands caught me. I stumbled as we moved and the room blurred, but then I was sitting down on the bench at the table and Clay was by my side. A plate appeared on the tabletop in front of me, slices of meat, a chunk of bread, and a few fruits arranged on it.

I closed my eyes, my stomach cramping with hunger while guilt badgered me, ordering me to get upstairs and back to work.

"Eat, Princess," Lars urged. "Please."

It'd be rude to let food go to waste like my tea often did.

I took a bite of the meat. And then another. And another, my hands bringing food to my mouth so fast, I was devouring it like I was starved.

Maybe I was.

Blinking, I looked around, feeling as if the lights had come back on around me, though nothing in the room seemed to have changed. But the lead weight in my chest seemed smaller, making it easier to breathe, and even if I still felt cold, my hands weren't shaking anymore.

Gods, how long had I gone without a real meal?

I glanced around to find the twins watching me.

"Better?" Clay asked.

"You want any more?" Lars added.

I shook my head. "No, thank you. I'm..." I drew a steadying breath. "That was excellent."

They nodded, still watching me, and discomfort began to prick at me again. What must I have looked like, ravenously tearing through that meal? Moreover, what was I doing here, resting, when I could be back at work trying to learn enough magic to maybe *do* something about this mess?

"I-I should get back to—"

"You're not alone, Princess," Lars interrupted gently.

"What?"

"Here. With this. With everything. You don't have to lock yourself away like you have been." He gave me a look like he hoped I'd understand. "None of us expect this to get solved overnight, okay?"

"I appreciate that, but—"

"You think we all haven't done this too?" Clay asked wryly.

I turned to him, confused.

"Worked ourselves ragged?" he continued. "Nearly collapsed from the need to do *something* to right the wrongs?"

He twitched his head toward his brother as if to encompass them both.

Lars nodded. "Once we got somewhere safe, after the..." He took a small breath. "After the Aneirans killed anyone they didn't take away, all we wanted to do was fix what had happened. But sometimes it doesn't work like that. You *want* it to. Something horrible happens, and you think if you just try hard enough, *push* yourself enough, you can make the world stop hurting and go back to the way it used to be. But... sometimes things take time."

My head shook. "I hear you, but I can't—"

"Lars and I barely knew magic from a hole in the ground when the Aneirans came," Clay interrupted.

I stopped. That couldn't be right. He conjured clothes from the gods knew where. Lars made dinners in an instant.

"Yeah, we, uh..." Clay chuckled, irony in the sound. "We didn't have much in the way of a *formal* education, back when we were kids. Just homeless street brats, him and me. But even when the society caretakers got their hands on us and tried to send us to school, we weren't the best students. He was better than I was." Clay nodded to his brother. "But neither of us cared much for sitting around staring at rocks all day when we could be out doing *literally* anything else."

Lars nodded, chuckling lightly too, but his smile didn't last long, turning into something sadder.

He was always so hopeful, and the change hurt to see.

"So you can imagine"—Clay's humor faded too—"how we felt a few years later when we couldn't stop the bastards tearing apart our city. Or when they came to the abandoned house where we lived with a couple other kids, and we couldn't save them either."

I glanced between the brothers, my heart aching for them. "Kids?"

Clay's smile was strained. "A few younger kids." He chuckled. "Still bigger than us, though. Giants and all. But... that made the Aneirans think they were adults. And that we were humans there with them. So they focused on the others, and when we tried to stop them, they knocked us out. Left us there while they hauled the rest away."

A breath escaped me.

"Those kids were our family," Lars said quietly. "We didn't really have one of our own, otherwise. Our parents were..." He gave a brief look to his brother. "Families are just people, right? One parent or ten. Doesn't matter when they're all just people in the end. Some are good. Some aren't. And ours..." He sighed. "Ours were very elite in Erenelle society, so having a kid who was 'defective' was simply intolerable, let alone *two*." He gestured between himself and his twin.

"Status didn't save them, though," Clay added. "When the Aneirans came..." He scoffed, no humor in the sound. "*They* had warning. Where we were, in that hovel, we'd only heard rumors that the Aneirans were launching a war against us. And it took the soldiers years to reach the capital anyway, and everyone kept thinking surely we'd turn them back. Stop them. But once they reached the city..." He shook his head. "We went back to check on our parents, just in case, but whatever defenses they'd had were useless. Aneirans burned their big old mansion to the ground. Chained up a few of them, we suspect. Killed the rest."

Lars pushed the plate aside and reached out, taking my

hand in both of his own. "We lost our birth family and our *real* family all within days of each other. So you can imagine how badly we wanted to get back at the Aneirans. How much we wanted to set things right."

"We didn't sleep or eat," Clay said. "We tracked them across miles of terrain, joining up with a few other survivors doing the same. And when we found them, we tried to break in and get our people, but..." He looked away, giving an odd shrug and scoff like it'd been a foolish idea in the first place.

Lars sighed. "There's a reason the seven of us are up here and not down there, sneaking in to break our people out. There's a reason we haven't mounted an attack in all these years."

A chill crept through me. "The Warden Wall."

His head tilted in acknowledgment. "And its smaller counterparts, all surrounding their camps."

I looked between them. The magic defenses surrounding the capital city were formidable. After my mother died, Father had asked Melisandre to do whatever she could to stop it from ever happening again.

The Warden Wall was the result. An invisible magic barrier much like the giants' own around the cabin, but this one surrounding all of Lumilia and—stories had it—horrifically deadly to giants. "But you both are..."

"Still here?" Clay joked.

I shivered and his smile faded. Exhaling briefly, he glanced at his brother, who rolled back his sleeve while Clay pulled up the edge of his sweater.

My eyes went wide. A gnarled scar circled Lars' wrist, as if a red-hot rope had wrapped around him. A larger scar twisted down Clay's side, like something had tried to chew straight into his flesh.

Discomfort flickering over his face, Clay tugged his sweater back into place.

"We were lucky," Lars said. "It didn't have as fast an effect on us as the other giants. With them, it..." He winced. "It tore into their bodies, turning them to blood and gristle and then dust, devouring them as they screamed. But something about the two of us... it slowed the magical impact. Gave me a few extra seconds to use what little I *did* know of magic to stop the effects from..."

"Killing us?" Clay offered wryly.

Lars looked away, a haunted look passing over his face, and his brother's gallows humor drained again.

I didn't know what to say, and on impulse I reached out, taking Lars' hand again and gripping Clay's arm as well. "I'm so sorry."

Clay gave me a rueful smile.

"You can't destroy yourself, Princess," Lars said. "You can't let the need to help drive you to the point where you're of no use to anyone, least of all yourself. If you let it, obsession will consume you. And what good would that do? How would that stop her? Our people *will* be free, and your father..."

He let out a breath, and I wondered if it pained Lars, saying anything about my father after everything Aneira and its king had put his people through.

But Lars only continued. "Your father *will* be avenged. But none of that will happen if you wear yourself out before the battle even begins."

"We've spent *years* trying to find a way around that wall, Princess," Clay said. "Every day, we're trying to think of ways to free our people. And we will. But we have to be alive and in good shape to do that, or we'll just end up dead like so many others who've tried." His mouth tightened. "So please. Maybe... take a break?"

I looked away. Their stories hurt, and their care did too. I wanted to make this better, and the idea of resting when the world felt like it was spiraling out of control...

"I can't let her get away with this," I said, my voice small in spite of myself.

"She won't." Clay reached up, swiping a tear from my cheek, and I realized I'd started crying. "Somehow, she won't."

His arm slid around my shoulders, and it was too much. A sob escaped me as the tears began to overwhelm my ability to shove them down.

Clay pulled me to his side, murmuring comfort as I cried.

"I have to stop her," I told him between sobs. "I *have* to."

Lars sank down on my other side. "You will."

Held between the two of them and encircled by their warmth, I could almost let myself hope the words were true.

Even after my tears slowed, I couldn't bring myself to move away from the table or the twins' sides. But then Lars shifted around, drawing me to my feet. "Come on, Princess."

"What?" I sniffled and glanced around. Clay was already by the door, and the plates were somehow gone from the table, taken in the time I'd been crying. Gently, Lars led me toward the hall. "Where are we going?"

"To sleep. You need it. We do too. We've been up for a while."

I hesitated. "I thought you said you couldn't sleep."

Again, they shared a look, and with the help of the food inside me, my brain finally clicked on the reason.

"You've been staying up in case I came downstairs, haven't you?"

They had the grace to look a tad embarrassed. "We've all been worried," Clay admitted with a shrug.

Air left me.

"It's late," Lars said. "Let's just get you to bed, okay?"

I shook my head. "No, I—"

"Please, Princess?"

The weight of protesting felt too heavy, as if everything from the past several weeks was bearing down all at once. In a blur, I followed them up the steps and then started for my room.

"No, no." Lars drew me toward a different door. "This way, come on."

I frowned. Sex? Now? Was that what this was? Yes, some distant part of my tired body still clamored to be with them, but the rest felt mired in cotton.

"Just sleep," Lars said as if reading something in my expression. "You need to rest, not to wake up and see those projects again."

The thought was heavy too. Every time I slept, I only had nightmares, and whenever I woke, the first thing I saw was the desk and all the things I still couldn't get to work. The dread of it all had settled like a leaden ball in my stomach, freezing me from the inside and dragging around with me wherever I went. How could he know that?

But then, from what he'd said, they'd been where I was too.

I followed him into his room. With a nod, he directed me toward his washroom past a door to my left, and I went.

Back home in Aneira, only the royal family had such luxuries. Here, each of the men did, and I did as well.

A few minutes later, I returned to find the large bed turned down and a fresh nightgown at the foot of it. By the door, Lars stood, Clay in the hall.

"We'll leave you to get some rest, then," Lars said.

A sound of protest left me. "Where will you sleep?"

"I'll stay with him down the hall." He nodded to his brother.

"No, no." I shook my head, everything feeling fuzzy. "I can't push you out of your room. I'll just…" I looked at the bed and then toward my bedroom. The thought of seeing everything I *couldn't* do again just ached. So did the fear of the nightmares that plagued me every night.

I didn't want to be alone right now, and the intensity of that left me shaking.

"Please?" I begged.

Clay and Lars shared a look, and then Lars notched his head slightly toward the bed.

"Might be a bit warm for her with all of us in here together," Clay argued quietly.

Warm? How could he say that? I shook my head, trying to think past the fog clinging to me. "No, it's… it's cold." A shiver rolled through me. "It's *so* cold."

The men paused. Lars glanced at his brother again, and Clay nodded as he shut the door.

They came toward me.

A tiny breath of relief left my chest. Neither said a word as Lars lifted the nightgown and nodded for me to take it. By the nightstand, Clay blew out the lamp.

The room plunged into darkness broken only by the thinnest line of moonlight slipping past the curtains. In the shadows, both men turned their backs, tugging off their sweaters and giving me privacy to strip off my dress and pull on the nightgown.

I hesitated, watching them, still enticed by them even with how tired I was. But sleep seemed to be their priority now, and so I'd do as they'd asked.

Turning my back as well, I put on the nightgown. It wouldn't keep me warm, that much was obvious. The silk fabric was deliciously thin, barely disguising the darker shadow of my nipples past its pale surface. But the thought that one of them had conjured this purely to see me in it made my insides melt toward liquid despite my exhaustion.

A rustle from the blankets made me turn back. Clay was in the bed, his back propped on the pillows, while Lars stood beside it and nodded for me to climb in. Their clothes were gone, with only a pair of undergarments covering them now, and I was struck speechless by the sight. Their bodies were muscled from years of mining and hauling ore back and forth from the caves to the cabin. The thin sliver of moonlight traced lines of silver and shadows across the plains and valleys of their torsos. Even without their distinctive scars, I could tell them apart. It was in how they held themselves—where Clay had an edge to his bearing like he'd cut someone with a word, Lars was as smooth and even as polished stone. The difference was subtle, yet as unique as a fingerprint.

Taking a steadying breath, I crossed to the side of the bed, though it brought me so enticingly close to Lars. But then, we were going to be closer still, weren't we?

I slipped between the sheets as Clay put an arm around me and drew me to his side. His skin felt so wonderfully warm, and his scent flooded my senses, fresh like summer and the sea. Behind me, the bed moved as Lars climbed in as well, pulling the blanket over us. His arm slipped around my side, his body spooning up behind me. His own delicious scent wrapped around me, similar to his brother's in a way —the heat of hot summer sand where Clay was the salty sea —laced with some indefinable spice that was purely *him.*

Relaxation stole over me, melting away the heaviness and the dread of my failures that had crushed me for so long. I only felt safe. In the shadows, I pressed a hand to Clay's chest as if I could immerse myself in his warmth and absorb it straight into my veins. At my back, Lars' hand stole down along my side to hold my hip, and I couldn't help how I rocked myself back against him.

A wordless sound of approval left him, but his fingers tightened on my hip as if to stop me. "You should get sleep, Princess."

I didn't listen, pushing against his bulge while I turned my head slightly, my lips finding Clay's chest. I curled my tongue around his nipple, and his breath hitched. "I'm so cold," I whispered.

The men were silent for a moment, and when I looked up, I saw Clay's blue eyes on his brother.

"Then let us fix that," Lars murmured.

Clay's hand took my jaw, drawing me upward, while Lars moved me to be positioned more on top of his twin. My lips landed on Clay's, his hands raking up through my hair to keep me with him as he deepened the kiss. Behind me, Lars slid his hands beneath my nightgown and up my sides to find my breasts.

Yes.

I made a pleading sound against Clay's lips while mois-ture soaked my core. I needed this. Them. Their warmth and comfort, and to feel them in me like Dex had been so many weeks before.

I needed them all.

Arching my back, I pushed my hips toward Lars, praying he'd understand what I craved. And a moment later, one of his hands left my breast to slide down between my legs and find the desire building there.

"Gods..." he murmured as his fingers circled my aching clit, and I moaned against his brother's lips. "Our girl's wet already."

Clay broke away from me. His eyes searched mine for a heartbeat, and then a grin spread across his face. Taking the front of my nightgown, his expression took on a decidedly wicked glint.

The nightgown and my underclothes disintegrated as if they had never been.

I gasped, suddenly naked between the two of them. Clay moved fast, drawing me back to him for a kiss while Lars shifted around behind me, messing briefly with a drawer on the nightstand and then doing something else I couldn't see. But his hands returned soon, positioning me while his brother plundered my mouth. Lars' fingers slid along my seam, back to my rear, and then teased around my other opening.

A thrill shot through me to feel him touching me there, and I broke away from Clay only long enough to look back at his brother. Lars spread something on his cock and then returned, massaging my opening as well. Hot desire pulsed through me as his finger slid in and out of me, working me open wider, and I moaned again. Clay reached down, gripping one of my breasts and never ceasing to kiss me, while his brother bent over me to kiss along my spine as he continued his ministrations.

I lost myself to the motions of their hands and mouths on me, only for my eyes to fly wide when I felt Lars move me again, pushing my legs wider and bringing me down closer to Clay's cock. As his own tip notched against my rear entrance, Lars leaned closer to my ear.

"Relax, sexy. We'll go slow."

I nodded, breathless. The sheer question of whether both of their enormous cocks could ever fit inside me at the same time was almost enough to send me over the edge, and as Lars began to enter me, I squeezed my eyes shut, a delicious mix of pleasure and pain twisting through me, inseparable and overwhelming.

"That's right," Clay murmured below me. His hand stole down between us, his fingers playing over my clit and stoking the exhilaration inside me higher. I opened my eyes to see him watching me. "You can do this, baby."

I wasn't sure about that, but I didn't want to stop. "More," I begged. "More."

Desire darkened the summer blue of his eyes, and behind me, a hungry noise left his brother. Lars' fingers dug into my side as he stretched me with his girth, sliding in farther, and the pain and pleasure of it made my entire body tingle. I'd be lucky if I could walk tomorrow, but gods, I didn't care. My pussy spasmed, desperate to be filled as well because this wasn't enough.

"Please," I whispered to Clay. "I want you in me when I come."

His eyes widened at my words, and then they flicked past me to his brother, checking in briefly. At whatever he saw, he pulled me closer, careful not to take me away from Lars, and his cock notched at my entrance.

"Please," I repeated.

Clay's lips curled. "You're going to be so full of us, we'll be dripping down your legs for days."

My whole body thrummed with desire, pleading for exactly that, and without another word, Clay pushed into me.

I gasped, my mouth falling open. His cock pressed against his brother's through my inner walls, and my eyes squeezed shut again at the incredible sensation. They were stretching me so much, it made pleasure mingle with pain, somehow creating a mixture that only left my body thrumming with craving for more.

"Take it, baby," Clay whispered to me. "Every inch of us."

I moaned, pushing back against them.

"That's it," Lars encouraged me. "Good girl."

"You're ours, Princess. Every part of you is ours."

I nodded, barely able to form words. "Yes, sirs."

Their hands tightened on me at my response, and Clay pushed into me harder. I could barely breathe at the feeling of them in the deepest parts of me. It hurt yet was amazing, and I couldn't sort out the confusing sensation.

Except to never want it to end.

Sheathed in me entirely, Clay paused only for a moment, and then slowly, both of them began a steady rhythm, drawing out of me only to thrust back in again.

Short cries of pleasure escaped me. I couldn't stay quiet, no matter how I tried. The thought flitted through my mind of what the other men might hear, and my eyes flew toward the door. Would they come to investigate?

Would they join us?

"Don't worry about the others, baby," Clay murmured like he'd read my mind. "Let them hear how good you feel."

Lars made a noise of agreement. "Let them hear how much our dirty, sexy good girl wants to be filled up with our cum."

My pulse flew higher at their words and frantic sounds of agreement came from me, wordless. I rocked between the twins, my entire being drawing down to their movements and the dark pleasure building inside me. To be claimed by them felt so right, as if having them with me was something I'd been waiting for all my life.

Because I *was* theirs. Somehow, I always had been, I just hadn't known it. And consenting to that claiming thrilled me in a way I couldn't describe.

My fingers dug into Clay's shoulders as I cried out with pleasure. Sweat built on my skin, the cold I'd felt for so long now a thing of the past. My breaths came in gasps as the two men moved within me, their hands on my hips and breasts. And when Lars' hand slipped around me to find my clit again, my orgasm overtook me so swiftly I lost the room in a blinding surge so strong I didn't know if my muscles even moved me anymore.

I *had* to be theirs, and as I rode the wave of my climax, nothing could have felt more right. I never wanted to come down.

Their hands clenched on me and the thrusting of their cocks became more desperate. Clay cried out beneath me as his own orgasm overtook him, and a heartbeat later, Lars' did the same, the hot rush of their passion surging into me.

Gods, yes.

I sagged down onto Clay as Lars pulled from within me

and rolled to one side. Clay's arms wrapped around my body, holding me to him while his cock twitched within me. Reaching over, Lars drew my face toward him and kissed me deeply, his tongue twisting with mine while his hand cupped my cheek.

"So good, baby," Clay murmured.

Lars drew back and nodded in agreement with his brother.

I smiled. Shifting around, Clay moved me between them and I nestled there in utter contentment. Dozy peace stole over me, making my eyes drift shut in the afterglow.

But I didn't mind. In this moment, there was nowhere else in the world I'd rather be than resting between two of my giants, wondering if maybe the bedroom door would open so that we could be joined by more.

17
MELISANDRE

I flinched back from the mirror as my spell upon the mountains suddenly sent up a flare. For weeks, there'd been no trace of her, and now only for a moment my spell had found... something.

Another flare followed. And another.

Exhilaration began to pound through me, and swiftly, I worked to bury any trace of it, along with any sign of how I'd been startled. I was still facing my mirror, and it was unwise to reveal too much emotion to those beings. They would only see it as an opportunity to strike.

"Show me," I commanded.

The Voidborn seethed beneath the surface for a moment, debating obeying me. I wasn't their master by any stretch of the imagination, but I knew the prospect of feeding would be too tempting for them to ignore.

The murky reflection cleared like smoke pulling back on all sides, and a bat's-eye view of the mountain slopes came into view. The thick pine forest fell away ahead, revealing an expansive clearing of unbroken snow.

And that was it. Just snow and the long shadows cast by the moon, with no sign of Gwyneira or prey or even a trail of red blood to break the endless white.

But *something* had sent up that flare.

At a flick of my fingers, the bat my spell rode swooped lower, heading for the clearing.

A flash of light erupted across the mirror, and then the view went dark.

But for just a moment, I caught a glimpse of a massive structure where before there had been only snow.

I exhaled, stepping back from the mirror. Clever. Powerful too. That defensive magic shielded something large enough to be a small castle in its own right. Doing that was no meager feat.

But my spell upon the mountains was intended to detect Gwyneira, and thus she was probably there.

With help.

"Surround them," I whispered.

A tingle spread over my skin as my magic twisted out through the ether, warping nature, bending and breaking it to my will.

"Don't let them escape the clearing."

18

GWYNEIRA

My eyes opened in the darkness, and for a moment, disorientation made me lie motionless. I wasn't in my bedroom, the unfinished work of learning magic glaring at me from the desk and hunger gripping my insides. Now someone warm was on either side of me, the sounds of their breathing soft while unfamiliar furniture filled the room, traced by moonlight.

Memories played back in enticing aches through my body, and a smile tugged at my lips. Clay and Lars. What we'd done together, despite how tired I'd been. After sex with the twins, I'd had no chance at resisting the need for rest.

But what had woken me now?

Not moving for fear of disturbing the men, I let my eyes slide over the room. Everything in the house was silent, leading me to suspect the hour was still late. Not even a creak of wood or whisper of air broke the quiet.

A chill crept over my skin.

My breath caught, dread stealing over me as if I were a

child certain the monster under my bed now prowled the room.

"Princess?" At Clay's whisper, I glanced over to find him watching me in the darkness. "What's wrong?"

I shook my head, returning my attention to the room. Had some frightful dream woken me, but I couldn't recall? Even now, my skin was crawling, not with cold but fear.

"I don't know," I whispered back. "Something—"

A shriek beyond the window shattered the silence. On the other side of me, Lars jolted awake.

"What the fuck?" Clay leapt from the bed, seeming to care nothing for the fact he was naked.

A flare of light came from outside.

In an instant, Lars was out of bed as well. Shaking, I followed, clutching the blanket to my breasts.

"Princess, stay back—"

Past the window, I saw a flash against the night sky, bright like a tiny star had exploded. Another followed with a piercing shriek, and then another and another still. Faster and faster they came, projectiles bursting at the edge of the clearing, and in the light, I could make out more shapes.

Bats. Hundreds upon hundreds of them, slamming into something that could only be the barrier, flaring bright and screaming as they burned and died.

"What is this?" I cried over the shrieking. "What's happening?"

Clay pulled me from the window. "Get Byron!" he yelled at his brother.

Lars raced from the room. With a swift gesture, Clay materialized clothes on us both, still watching the window as if bracing for it to break.

I shivered in the breeches, sweater, coat, and boots that

had manifested themselves on my body as if I'd been wearing them the whole time. Now that we were out of the bed and every ounce of tranquility had fled, the cold inside me was back, shaking me like a leaf in the wind. That was magic out there. It had to be.

And I had no question in my mind about to whom it belonged.

Byron appeared at the door, Lars on his heels wearing clothes he must have created on the run. Roan and Niko were behind them, while from down the corridor, I heard Dex shout. "What the hell is going on?"

"Something's forcing them to do that," Niko gasped, staring around in horror like he could see straight through the walls. "They... *Gods,* they don't want to..."

"Can they get through?" Roan demanded.

No one answered as Byron strode to the window. His eyes darted over the bats still striking the barrier, and then he lifted his hands, saying something low and fast that I couldn't understand.

An odd sensation passed over my skin, like the tingling in the air an instant before a lightning bolt crackled across the sky. It rolled up through the ground, past me and toward him.

"Niko?" he snapped over his shoulder. "Help them?"

The younger man crossed the room to him quickly. Putting a hand to the windowsill, he closed his eyes and began murmuring under his breath, his face tightening like he was fighting something.

"She'll be coming," Dex told the group at large.

The air fled my lungs, but the others only looked grim.

"Five minutes," he continued.

"I'll check the defenses downstairs," Roan said before taking off for the first floor.

"Lars," Dex said. "Secure the cellar."

The man nodded and raced away.

I watched him go. The cellar? Why would he need to secure that when there were countless windows and at least two doors to worry about?

Dex cast a glance at Byron. "Five minutes," he repeated, his gaze flicking to Niko.

Byron nodded. By the window, Niko didn't react, his attention locked on the creatures outside and whatever spell he was casting in an attempt to save them.

But the explosions of light against the barrier seemed to be slowing. I prayed that was because he was succeeding and not just because the colony was running out of bats.

Dex looked at us. "Go."

With his arm still around my shoulder, Clay brought me with him out of the room. My body ached every bit as much as I'd expected it would, my hips and legs throbbing from what the twins and I had done, but I gritted my teeth, not letting myself slow down. Hurrying down the stairs, I followed the others along the hall on the first floor.

Ozias was already by the front door, and my breath stopped when I saw the massive weapon in his hands. It was larger, even, than the ones I'd seen him carry before, like an axe met a scythe and had a monstrous child. The enormous blade was carved with intricate markings, and its edge glinted strangely in the light, like the darkness of the metal was picking and choosing what flecks of light to send back. In his hand, the gnarled, carved handle was thick as a tree branch and nearly as tall as me. A shorter blade was strapped to his back, more runes on the weapon and the same dark metal shining oddly in the lantern light.

Clay didn't pause. Turning before we came near the front door, he pressed a hand to an otherwise unremarkable stretch of wall. A *thunk* sounded inside the wood and a door swung open beside me, revealing a staircase leading down. Firelight glimmered against stone at the bottom.

"Come on," Clay said.

I balked. "What is this?"

"Exit strategy. We need to get away from the house. The queen will be coming."

I looked between him and Ozias, implications hitting me. "If she is, then she's coming for me. If I run, you all could be safe."

Ozias cast a look over his shoulder at me and I couldn't read his expression. It seemed... horrified.

"Princess—" Clay started.

I took a step back. "What if she comes here and destroys this place? I can't let you lose your home."

"We'll take the house down," Clay replied like it was obvious.

I blinked, not sure how to wrap my mind around that. But even if they could do that, the idea was awful on some level. Would that kill the energy that made this place almost alive? "No. I'll just leave. You won't have to—"

"No." Ozias' deep voice cut me off.

I looked over at him in alarm. He'd barely said a word to me since finding me in the woods weeks before. "I can't let you destroy this beautiful—"

In two strides, Ozias cut across the distance between us. Coming to a stop only inches from me, his massive hand encircled my arm as if to haul me bodily down the stairs. His eyes burned down into mine, and for a heartbeat, I had the impression I was looking at a wild animal, not a man.

He froze, his nostrils flaring, and then he drew a sharper breath, like he'd scented something on me. Irrationally, I wondered if he could smell some trace of what Clay, Lars, and I had done.

A low growl emanated from him, a possessive note in the sound that made my insides quiver. His lips twitched, pulling back from his teeth as if baring them in a snarl.

"Oz, chill," Clay said.

For a heartbeat, the man didn't move, and then slowly his gaze dropped from mine.

But not before I caught a flash of pain in his eyes.

"Princess," Clay continued, watching Ozias as much as me. "Our merry band of misfits here might just be the last free giants in the world, so there's not a chance in hell the queen will leave us alone if she finds us. And before you think that if you hadn't come here, it wouldn't be like this" —he gave a wry chuckle—"that bitch is probably searching everywhere for you. If she wasn't, she wouldn't have sent bats as scouts. She'd already be on our doorstep herself." He nodded toward the outside, not taking his attention from either of us. "This would've happened regardless."

Pain crushed down on my chest anyway. I'd lost my home. Now they were losing theirs too.

"She'll have her Huntsmen bring swords made of hammered ore," Clay continued. "They'll attack the barrier, and eventually it'll fall, so we need to get the fuck out of here."

He eased a hand between me and Ozias, watching the other man as much as me, and carefully drew me toward him.

Ozias released me. My hand tingled, blood returning after the force of his grip.

Clay brought me with him toward the steps.

"What about the others?" I asked.

"They'll be coming. But we have to go. Please."

At a loss, I followed him down the stairs. A cellar of mortar and stone stretched out several dozen yards from me on either side, and to my left, Lars waited by another stretch of seemingly unbroken wall.

Clay jerked his chin at his brother and the man moved quickly, touching a combination of places on the stone.

A space of wall vanished like a dream, and a dark tunnel waited beyond it. In the light from the basement, I could only make out a row of unlit lanterns hanging from metal hooks on the tunnel wall, after which there was nothing but shadows.

At my alarmed glance, Clay winked at me. "Miners always make sure they have another way out."

Footsteps on the stairs made me turn. Dex and Roan descended the steps, packs on their backs and in their arms as well. They handed the bags out to the others swiftly while Byron, Niko, and Ozias descended after them. Closing the door, Byron held his hands to it, again saying something that I couldn't understand. An odd feeling twisted across me a second time, like electricity ghosting through the air, past me to him.

"What's he doing?" I asked.

"Protection spells." Clay brought me with him toward the gaping hole in the wall. "Come on."

Anxiety filled me as we approached the tunnel, but the others didn't seem nervous at all. Lars held out a hand toward the lanterns, and at a murmured word from him, the wicks inside flared to life. Not reacting to the display of power in the slightest, Dex simply took a lantern down and started off with utter certainty.

"Princess." Byron came up to me and extended a hand. On his palm rested a pendant of ore that reflected shades of gold and silver in the light, all of it wrapped in wire and strung on a black ribbon. "For protection. Once we're beyond the barrier, we can't risk whether she'll be able to track you more easily."

Trepidation swirled like a swarm of bees in my stomach and I trembled as he looped the ribbon over my head. My fingers reached up, turning the pendant around. It felt warm against my skin, as if even the slight heat clinging to it from his hand was discernible when my body still felt so cold.

"Thank you," I said.

Byron nodded, giving me a smile as he clasped a hand to my arm in a reassuring gesture.

It helped.

Taking a steadying breath, I followed the others into the tunnel. When we were all inside, Byron turned and pressed his palm to the wall.

The opening sealed itself completely, like there'd never been a door there at all.

"Sixty yards out," Ozias said, his low voice like a rumble from the earth itself.

No one else commented on the strange statement.

Firelight from the lanterns played across walls of dirt and stone as we hurried through the tunnel, the serpentine path twisting beneath the earth. I couldn't hear anything from the world above, and nothing changed of the darkness behind us. If not for the curves in the tunnel, I would have thought we were walking while standing still, so little seemed to change around us.

But then Ozias stopped.

Turning, he watched the tunnel behind us like he was staring straight through the rock to the world above.

"Come on," Clay said, urging me past him with a hand on my back to keep me moving. "Stay clear, okay?"

I did as he instructed. With a confirming glance that I was staying put, Clay rejoined the others.

"Here goes," he muttered.

They extended their hands toward the ceiling, and the strange tingling feeling that had passed me when Byron closed the tunnel entrance earlier suddenly grew a thousandfold. A bizarre sensation stirred in my middle in response, like something was swirling there. The feeling built and spread, passing into the cold rock and out into something warm. Something alive.

Something that extended up from the earth into the air above. It now heard its master calling, and so it came.

The stone around me shivered. I could feel that strange energy pouring back into the earth, diffusing through the dirt and rock, the power that was once so firm and solid now melting into the ground.

Breathless, I stared up at the tunnel ceiling. It was the house. Everything of the house returning to the earth. But how could I feel this, when I couldn't feel any magic when I tried to do it on my own? The sensation was monumental. Overwhelming. I wanted to retreat, as if it would flood through the very rock above us and fill the tunnel until we drowned in its energy.

But when the last of it had passed into the stone and

dirt, the energy seemed to settle, fading into stillness as if falling asleep.

The men lowered their arms. I stared at them.

"That was…" I couldn't find a word. "You took down the house, didn't you?"

Byron looked back at me. "You felt that?" His tone didn't make it a question. More of a confirmation.

Yet, honestly, of what? So I'd felt it. I couldn't *do* magic.

Uncomfortable, I avoided his gaze. "So is it all gone now?"

Clay shrugged as he came back toward me. "It's just energy sleeping in the earth. We can bring it back."

I nodded, somehow relieved. Weeks ago, the prospect of a living house terrified me. Now I felt like destroying it would be akin to putting down a loyal guard dog. Horrible, and to be avoided at all costs.

And as for the *power* that'd taken…

Gripping my hand, Clay kept me with him as the others started off. I followed, though I couldn't stop myself from looking back at the tunnel behind us as I went. I knew what they'd told me about the house, that they'd made it. But what I'd felt…

Gods, my people said the giants were powerful. That was supposedly the reason Aneira needed my stepmother's magic to defend us against them. And to be sure, I hadn't thought the giants weak. But *that*…

I couldn't make a barrier the size of a melon. Hell, I couldn't control a trace of magic at all. Compared to their power, what good was I here?

I hurried along the tunnel after the giants, discomfort lodged inside me like a lead weight. The men had never indicated my ability—or utter lack of it—mattered to them.

And I knew what Clay had said. Maybe he was even right that my stepmother would have found them regardless.

But she wouldn't have been looking out here in the first place if not for me. And in the face of such power and peril, what was I truly offering these wonderful men?

Except for the risk that one or all of them would be locked up or killed?

19
MELISANDRE

In the darkness on the mountainside, my body shifted back to human form as I set down upon the slope, a flurry of snow swirling from my arrival. Ahead, dead bats lay in a circle around the clearing, their wings motionless and their necks snapped. That much death should have fueled my spell to a dizzying strength, giving it enough power to overcome whatever defense the fools in the clearing had sought to raise.

But something had fought me for them. Something that fractured my hold enough to send the remnants of the flock fleeing into the night sky.

I'd never known the Jeweled Coven to care for bats.

I walked forward as, behind me, my vampire servants landed as well, shifting back and trailing me like dogs on a leash. Human soldiers would be coming in a few hours, trudging along the ground like the maggots they were. But my vampires and I had flown here at high speed, and no one should have been able to flee this place fast enough to escape us without being seen.

My eyes flicked down. Beyond the bats, a line of depressions cut through the snow all the way down to the earth below, as if something had lain here. Numerous somethings, all of them roughly round in shape and circling the clearing as well.

The witches' defense most likely. But it was gone now, as if the earth itself had swallowed it back up, and the blowing snow around us was well on its way to erasing the signs of their presence entirely.

I murmured spells beneath my breath as I extended a hand toward the boundary line.

Nothing.

"You," I snapped over my shoulder at my servants. Several looked between themselves for a moment before they drew back, leaving only the one standing nearest to me.

"Y-yes, Mistress?" The man wrung his splotched apron in his grimy hands, the discolored fabric still in place from when he'd served as a cook in the castle, years before, though now it was stained with blood from when I allowed him to have a kill. His sallow face hadn't improved with death, and his wheedling voice still grated. I'd killed him for being an annoyance and turned him for the amusement of seeing his family cry every time he was spotted as a "ghost" on the castle grounds. Of course, they'd finally fled, traumatized by the sightings, leaving him pointless.

He'd hardly be missed.

I waved a hand at the space between the trees. "Check the clearing."

The man hesitated, casting a look at his companions before slowly walking forward. At the line of bats, he faltered.

An irritated sound escaped me and I snapped my fingers,

sending a whip of magic lashing toward him. The blow struck, flinging him past the bats and into the clearing.

Shaking, he climbed to his feet, looking around as clumps of disturbed snow fell from his ragged clothes. "What now, Mistress?"

My eyes narrowed. Stepping forward, I lifted my feet carefully over the row of dead bats.

The clearing was unchanged.

With a low growl of frustration, I walked across the snow. There had been a structure here. I had seen it. But now, barring the depressions where the barrier stones had been, nothing remained to show anyone had ever been here at all. The wind was stronger at the heart of the clearing, blowing snow across the terrain and wiping away any disturbed drifts. Not even a brick or stone lingered on the white expanse.

Turning in a slow circle, I surveyed the clearing. Those pesky witches of the Jeweled Coven thought they could escape me. They thought they could protect her from what was coming.

My lips peeled back from my fangs as I extended my hands over the ground and murmured spells that would be even more powerful now that I was here in the mountains themselves, rather than at a distance in the castle.

Even if they tried to keep Gwyneira from me, it wouldn't matter. Even if they attempted to break my grip on nature, it wouldn't be enough. She couldn't be far, not with the speed at which I'd arrived here.

And if she hadn't turned already, all I needed was to nudge her over the precipice into death for all my plans to be fulfilled. The closer she came to dying, the more my power over her would take hold.

My enemies thought to resist me.
They were about to learn what fools they'd truly been.

20

GWYNEIRA

After what felt like miles and miles, we finally left the tunnel and emerged into the night.

"So," I asked, watching the mountains warily, "where are we going now?"

"There are some caves to the north." Dex held up his lantern, scanning the pine trees and slopes of unbroken snow with a look in his eye like he was running a thousand strategies through his mind. "Come on."

Surrounded by the men, I continued walking. The snow was thick around my feet, but I barely felt the cold. Exhaustion, though. That dragged at me as time continued on. Moving my feet through the white fluff was infinitely tiring, and my body still ached from last night, not to mention all the sleepless nights before it. I longed to stop, slow down, perhaps rest for a time.

Birds called in the distance, their cries faint and thready over the mountainsides. Were they like the bats, trapped in my stepmother's thrall and scouring the slopes for any trace of us? Regardless, whatever adrenaline remained in my body flooded my veins with every cry, reminding me that we couldn't pause, if not for my safety, then for the safety of all the men around me.

But it was hard going. The forest was thick, and the darkness felt like a living thing lurking just beyond the reach of our lights. Even the others began to look tired after a time, their heads shaking as if to clear their minds of the urge to sleep and remind themselves of why we needed to keep moving.

After what felt like an eternity, though, a cave finally came into view. Its mouth was stark against the white snow and seemed to swallow the light from our lanterns. Evergreen trees stood nearby, sheltering it from the worst of the bitter wind, and relief flooded me at the thought we could pause, if only for a time.

The men seemed to feel the same way. Grateful noises escaped them, and their steps accelerated as they approached the cave opening.

"Roan, help Clay gather some wood for a fire," Dex ordered. "Lars, you think you could make us anything?"

Lars nodded, though he looked exhausted by the proposition. Roan and Clay headed off to do as asked.

"Cave clear, Niko?" Dex continued to the younger man.

Niko glanced at Ozias and twitched his head. With Ozias gripping his axe ahead of him, Niko lifted his lantern and ventured into the cave.

My body ached. All I wanted was to lie down. But now that we'd paused, other necessary things pushed at me. "Um, I'm going to go..." I nodded toward a cluster of trees.

Dex extended his lantern to me and I took it. "Stay close," he said. "We've gone miles from where she was using her magic to find you, but we still need to be careful. Byron, would you put a few pieces of ore around the area, just in case?"

The man was already reaching for the contents of his bag.

I trudged back through the snow, though everything in me begged to go back and just lie down. My bladder wanted my attention, though, and tiredly, I set to letting it have its way. At least I was no more cold than normal, even outside in the snow. I'd be in the cave soon, and there'd be a fire and food.

Finished, I pulled my breeches back into place and reclaimed my lantern. Weaving past the trees, I bent as I navigated around the branches of the dense forest.

Something brushed my neck. My pendant plopped into the snow.

Confused, I put a hand to the back of my neck as I looked behind me, lifting the lantern to see better.

Nothing was there. Just the endless drifts and trees all around me.

Confused, I turned back and bent down, retrieving the pendant. Alarm spread through me at the sight of the silk ribbon.

It was cut as neatly as if by a pair of scissors.

"What the...?" I whispered.

I started to rise and something caught my hair, raking across my scalp. Hissing with pain, I froze. What the hell? Twisting carefully, I tried to look back to see what had caught me.

A gnarled vine extended from the pine at my side, suspended in midair between me and the tree.

I blinked. I would have sworn that hadn't been there a moment before.

Moving slowly so as not to rip it from my hair, I set my lantern down and then reached up to untangle the bramble.

The twigs only stabbed deeper, pricking my scalp like the tines of a sharp comb. Startled, I dropped the pendant again, a small cry of alarm escaping me.

My vision swirled.

"Princess?" Byron's voice came from beyond the trees.

I opened my mouth to respond, but I couldn't seem to find my voice. My throat was strangely thick, and a heavy feeling stole over my body, as if all my muscles were turning to mud. The ground rolled beneath me and I staggered, struggling to keep my feet as the painful pinpricks in my scalp began to burn.

Footsteps thudded in the distance, but the tossing of the mountainside became too much. Cold snow caught my cheek as I hit the ground. Beyond the lantern before me, I could see blurry shapes running, but with every passing second, they faded farther down the long tunnel of night.

Everything went dark.

21

CLAY

My arms full of firewood, I cursed the damn snow as an icy patch of ground threatened to take my feet from under me. The sooner we got somewhere we could create the cabin again, the happier I'd be.

I'd gotten a lifetime's worth of living rough in my childhood and the years following the destruction of our nation. Now, I wanted a real bed and a fire I didn't have to tend myself.

"You think this cave is far enough from the cabin?" Roan asked beside me as he stepped over a fallen log. Up ahead, the cave mouth came into view.

I shrugged. "I think the queen's got a whole mountain range to contend with, and we could have gone in any direction. We can at least stay the night before—"

Niko raced from the cave opening, his eyes wide and his face a picture of horror.

Oh, shit. "What's wrong?"

"The forest. It's—"

"Gods of the Stone, no!"

Byron's cry sent a spike of fear straight through my heart. In an instant, I dropped the firewood and bolted toward the sound, swearing at the icy terrain as it tried to slow me down.

"What is it?" Lars called behind me. "What's happened?"

I skidded around a cluster of trees and a nightmare met my eyes. Gwyneira was on the ground, her eyes closed. Byron was crouched over her, saying spells so fast his words were an urgent, pleading blur.

"Niko, get over here," he snapped between lines.

The young man rushed closer and I followed. A bramble was caught in her hair, the tiny branches along its length sunk so tightly between her dark locks that blood glinted in the lantern light. Meanwhile, the pendant that was supposed to protect her lay on the snow at her side, the ribbon cut as if something had sliced it in two.

Footsteps came from behind me. Gasps left the others as they saw Gwyneira.

"No one touch anything," Dex ordered. "Look at the tree."

I tore my eyes from the princess. The evergreen beside her was totally ordinary, except for the gnarled vine tangled up through it. The damn thing was almost unnoticeable, hidden between the branches, except for one long piece that extended like a knobby finger to catch Gwyneira's hair.

And the vine wasn't even *kind of* okay.

Virulent green sap dripped from the rough surface, glinting in our lantern light and steaming in the cold winter air.

"Can you charm it, Niko?" Dex asked.

The younger man crouched down, his eyes on the

gnarled vine. "I've never seen anything like this, but I can try."

He extended his hands, murmuring rapid spells under his breath. The branch twitched and trembled like an animal, almost as if it was trying to fight him.

Ozias muttered a curse under his breath.

Tugging aside my winter coat, I ripped a piece of cloth from the shirt beneath my sweater. Crouching down beside him, I wrapped the fabric around my hand. "You got that thing?" I asked him.

Niko grimaced, but he nodded.

From the corner of my eye, I saw Dex motion to Lars. My brother circled us.

"Ready?" I asked him, not taking my eyes from the vine.

He nodded too.

I watched Niko and the vine.

"Go," he said.

With my wrapped hand, I grabbed at the least sap-covered portion of the thing I could see.

The vine flinched back, evading my grasp and tugging on Gwyneira's hair as it moved. She moaned with pain, her eyes still closed.

Behind me, Roan swore.

Dex crouched beside me, grabbing Gwyneira's arms. "Go again," he ordered. "One... two..."

I snagged the vine and ripped it away from Gwyneira at the same moment Dex pulled her away from the tree. Releasing the branch quickly, I hissed as the sap began eating through the cloth covering my hand. I tore the fabric off and tossed it aside as the vine twisted and searched back and forth in midair like a tentacle.

"Lars," Dex snapped.

My brother extended his hands. Niko and Byron retreated while heat built in the air like somebody had opened a gateway to the sun.

The vine burst into flames. Before our eyes, it crumbled away, falling as gray ash from the tree to coat the snow.

A shudder rolled through me, and absently, I rubbed my hand, checking that no trace of that sap had touched me.

"Is she okay?" Roan called, hanging back from our group with his arms wrapped around his middle like he was holding something inside. His eyes were fixed on Gwyneira, though, and he looked damn near beside himself with worry.

Byron pressed a hand to the princess's face, saying something fast beneath his breath. Gwyneira murmured and stirred, her brow furrowing, but her eyes didn't open.

"We need to get her back to the cave," Byron said. "I can—"

"What the hell?" Roan cried.

I looked back at him to see him pointing, and when I followed his gesture, horror shot through me all over again.

Where the branch's sap and ash had fallen on the snow, a fog was rising. Twisting around like a ghost of the limb itself, the misty tentacle whipped straight toward Gwyneira.

But it shot past her, slamming into Byron and Niko and propelling them both away from her. As I raced toward the princess, the ghostly branch returned, wrapping around her like a snake.

She lurched on the ground. The column of smoke tightened around her chest, crushing in on her like a corset from hell. Her mouth moved, clearly gasping for air.

But she couldn't breathe.

"Gods, it's killing her!" Niko cried, scrambling upright.

"Move!" Ozias yelled.

I looked back and then retreated fast. With a roar, Ozias swung his axe over his head and slammed it down into the foggy branch. The magical blade ripped through the limb, and the mist flew apart like smoke in a hurricane, dissipating into nothing.

Ozias grunted contemptuously.

I raced to Gwyneira's side. Her chest rose and fell with rapid gasps and her eyes moved beneath her lids.

"Princess?" I pressed a hand to her cheek. "Come on, baby. Please, wake up."

She made a pained noise.

"Byron?" Dex called. "Niko? You okay?"

I glanced up in time to see the red-haired man push to his feet. "Yes. Damn thing didn't care about anything but getting to her."

Wordlessly, Niko nodded.

More anger than pain on his face, Byron returned to the princess's side. With a quick glance over her, he reached back into his bag and pulled out a vial of glistening black liquid. Holding it up before his eyes, he muttered something in the old tongue, though I only knew the sound, not a damn word of what he said.

Blue light flared inside the bottle like a tiny star. Swiftly, he uncorked the top and then parted Gwyneira's lips, pouring the liquid carefully into her mouth.

"Come on," he murmured. "Please, Princess."

She swallowed hard and then gasped, her eyes flying open. Blinking, she looked around, confusion on her face at the sight of all of us. "W-what happened?"

Relief just to hear her speak nearly sat me down in the snow.

"Dark magic," Byron said.

"That bitch queen," Ozias elaborated in a grumble.

My heart still pounding, I helped the princess to her feet, keeping a hand on her to hold her steady—and to reassure myself she was still here. Byron shoved the bottle back into his bag and then snagged the pendant from the snow as well.

Gwyneira gripped my arm tightly and turned, looking back at the tree and then at the ashes still on the snow, speckled with her blood. Trembling, her hand lifted to touch her hair, and she winced at the wound there.

Gods, I hated to see her in pain.

I glanced over at the others, seeing similar looks on their faces to what was probably on mine. Something inside me would rather that damn branch have stabbed me a thousand times than hurt her once. And the fact the queen had to be behind this?

Damn me, it felt like we'd failed Gwyneira.

Roan turned away first, walking back toward the cave as if trying to put distance between himself and us. Ozias shifted his weight, seeming uncomfortable, and headed off into the forest while Niko wouldn't quite meet anyone's eyes.

"We need more defenses," Lars said. "A lot more."

Byron nodded. "Agreed. More distance as well. If the queen's power could reach her here..."

I felt Gwyneira tremble again. In the lantern light, her skin appeared so bloodless, and her chest rose and fell with tiny breaths, like she couldn't get more air in her lungs. A few more minutes and only the gods knew what would have happened.

Bending, I lifted her up into my arms and she gave a

small gasp. But her arms wrapped around me, keeping me close, and she nestled against my chest.

Determination settled in my gut like a ball of stone. We couldn't lose her. *I* couldn't. "Come on," I said, holding her tight. "Let's get you out of here."

22

MELISANDRE

"Damn!" I slammed a hand to the cave floor, and beyond the rough shelter, trees died for twenty feet around. Whirling, I glared at my servants, all of them cowering in terror in the shadows.

I'd *had* her. Mere seconds more and no one could have saved her.

And instead...

A snarl escaped me as I stalked back into the shadows of the cave, away from the first light of the burning day. Whoever was helping her was more resourceful than I thought. A magical defense protecting an entire clearing was vastly different than what it took to overcome the intricate spellwork I'd just employed. Yet they'd done both.

Could she have more than the Jeweled Coven assisting her?

Grinding my teeth, I glared at the stone walls trapping me now that the sun had risen. No matter. Even if she wasn't dead yet, she'd been perilously close several times, and every brush with mortality brought her closer to the edge of turning. The changes would be subtle, at least at first. A chill no matter the warmth around her. Hunger she could never satisfy. But soon... oh, soon, they'd be undeniable.

A strange sensation whispered through my mind like a whimper in the distance, and my lips curled. Her nascent connection to my will was already coming into existence, binding her as my pawn after all these years. When it came to fruition, the bond would guide me to her, and her to me, and then nothing would stop my will from being done.

I turned back, looking out on the daylight beyond the cave. The surviving forest waited amid snow and ice, a tangle of bushes and evergreens and trees that in summer might even flower or bear fruit.

The words of the spell slipped from me effortlessly, and I could feel the threads of the spellwork twisting out past the dead trees and the tangled forest.

Seeking its target.

I smiled. "Not much longer now, Gwyneira. Not much longer at all."

23
GWYNEIRA

No one wanted to stay anywhere near the tree, and that meant the cave was no longer an option. Without a word, the men gathered their things and then continued onward, weaving a path up through the snow toward another cave they said was higher on the mountainside. Wintry wind whipped around us, tugging my hair as surely as that branch had done. The trees thinned and then disappeared entirely, leaving us on barren slopes looking out on a world impossibly distant below. The air was thin—not that I could seem to draw a deep breath of it. I couldn't feel the cold at all. Or anything of the world around me, for that matter, except for the dull pain of my ribs and the sharp pain on my scalp.

And Clay's arms.

I snuggled tighter into him. On any ordinary day, I would insist I could walk. But right now, when the world was made of numb ice and even the air in my lungs felt alien, he was warm and safe and real in a way I needed as surely as the sun in the sky.

We reached the next cave as the last pink and gold traces of dawn burned away into the crisp blue of day. As Lars charmed a fire into existence without a word, Byron set to putting up defenses on the mouth of the cave. Ozias left immediately, growling that he'd scout the area, and Roan followed a moment later without saying a single thing. It wasn't until Dex and Niko had arranged a pile of blankets on the floor that Clay finally lowered me down.

I extended my hands toward the fire, wishing I could absorb more of its warmth. My skin was paler than I remembered, somewhere between the blush of life and the color of snow, and the sight made me tremble.

That vine had nearly killed me. I knew it as clearly as my own name.

"Why is this happening?" I whispered, watching the dancing flames.

Quiet fell around me and I looked up to see the men glancing at each other.

"What do you know of the queen's history, Princess?" Byron asked quietly.

I hesitated, a flutter of fear in me for the odd question. "What do you mean?"

His brow rose as if in silent repetition of the question.

I blinked, searching for a response. "I know she was..." I hesitated, amending my words. "I know she *claimed* to be my mother's friend from many years ago. And that she came to our castle the day she also claimed that giants killed my mother." A small breath left me at how many things, in the end, only amounted to her stories with no other evidence. "I know she was secretive, but she always said it was for our protection. That the forces she wielded would drive mad those inexperienced in the magical arts." My eyes returned to the merry blaze only a few feet away, each flame conjured by magic. "And I know she lied."

Silence followed my words for a moment.

"What do you know of the Witch War?" Byron continued.

A chill rolled through me. "Not much. Only what anyone else knows, I suspect."

The scholarly man made a soft sound as if he wasn't surprised. "May I tell you a story?"

I twitched my head in agreement, still watching the flames. Clay stayed at my side, his arm around me, while the sounds of grit and gravel shifting came from nearby as the others sat down around the fire. I looked up to see them regarding me through the flames.

"Once upon a time," Byron continued in the careful tones of someone relaying a wealth of information as concisely as he could. "There was a great coven of witches. They were drawn from every kingdom and from all walks of life, and they were united in one purpose: to protect the lands. They kept peace and averted war. With their power, they always helped those who came to them for aid." A sad smile crossed his face. "They were the truest sign of the peaceful times this world once enjoyed. They were called the Jeweled Coven.

"But as the years went on, some among their number grew discontent. To serve the world when you have such power requires wisdom and a strength of character that, sadly, some of them did not possess. They wanted to rule instead."

He sighed. "Dark forces exist out there, Princess. Powers more terrifying than many witness in their worst night-mares. Some of these ravenous forces are called the Voidborn, and they live between the realms, lingering in the empty spaces that divide this world—indeed, this entire *reality*—from a multitude of others. Only the greatest of magic users have ever seen this space, and fewer still have glimpsed the places that lie beyond it. But these dark forces care nothing for that. Life is an abomination to them. They wish it destroyed in the effort to expand their own power. Their hunger is without end, and the truth is that even if all of life fell to them, they would only turn on themselves, shredding and feasting and killing until nothing was left."

I shivered.

"But the power of life itself repels them and keeps them from reaching us, and so it's only with help they're able to extend their influence into this world. They seek people who would do their work for them, and they offer much in return —though everything comes with a price."

He stirred the flames with a branch. "I was far too young to see the Witch War myself, but after my parents died, I grew up as a servant to the monks of the Order of Berinlian where great magic users of Erenelle studied." A soft chuckle left him. "I was small and useful for tasks that required getting into tight spaces. But several of the scholars took me under their wings, despite how different from them I appeared. That's where I learned the beginnings of what I know of magic." The smile faded into something sadder. "Before I lost him to the Aneiran War, my most trusted mentor, Dathan, used to tell me stories of the Witch War. He spoke of this group of discontented witches who banded together in secret, forming a dark coven all their own. They summoned these forces, pledging their souls to the Void-born in exchange for unimaginable power to rule the world as they saw fit. But even with their offerings, their newfound gifts were not without a steeper cost. In the grip of these powers, the witches were transformed and their humanity was stripped from them. They became creatures of the night who would burn in the sun. Beings who could feel neither cold nor heat, who had no heartbeat nor breath in their lungs, but who could compel others by the force of their will and magic alone.

"They became vampires."

Around the fire, several of the others shifted uncomfortably.

"After this, these witches returned to the leaders of Jeweled Coven, intent on claiming leadership, but all the coven opposed them. Dathan said that the battle raged so fiercely, the flares and blasts of their magic in the western mountains could be seen from Erenelle itself, like a deadly storm of a thousand colors seething on the horizon. By the time it was done, the very nations of the mountains had been devoured by the destruction, and the great seat of magic in this world was destroyed, possibly forever. In the end, the witches of the Jeweled Coven were gone and no one knew for certain if any had survived." He paused, his green eyes meeting mine. "Until your mother returned."

My breath caught.

"Stories differ on how she escaped. Some say she was thrown into a river and swept away from the carnage. Others claimed the vampire witches left her for dead, or that her strength was enough to hold her enemies back until she could get away. But whatever the story, your mother survived one of the greatest magical battles seen in a thousand years, and rather than hide or break, she chose to step right back into the open as the queen of Aneira and work to maintain peace in a different way."

He glanced at the others. "Most of us remember little of those days, as we were only children at the time, but we know they were peaceful. Disputes were settled with treaties and agreements for trade, not swords and blood. Borders were places of easy passage, not barricades to trap people inside as easily as keep them out." A fond smile crossed his face. "As a young child, I recall traveling across half a dozen nations with the monks, trading gems for books and scrolls for our mountain archives, and none of them barred us passage or threatened us in any way." The happy memory seemed to fade. "But then your mother died."

Running his hands back and forth over his thighs, he sighed. "There was no border war between our people, no matter what the stories now say. Our people did not kill your mother over 'ancestral lands.' But like all great lies, it started as a twisting of the truth. Your people had found an old map with a quarter-mile difference in the border across one small field in the north of your country, and so our kingdoms were engaged in a mutual academic project to determine when and why the border shifted. Neither side was fighting over it. It was a rocky field that couldn't even grow crops well. And while, yes, wars *now* have been fought over far less, at the time, it was something of a joke."

He shook his head sadly. "In the days after your mother died, the entire world changed. Our people were blamed. Imprisoned. Enslaved. Your stepmother rose up, taking her place at your father's side. Around the kingdom, the homeless and helpless began to go missing. Most were never seen again. A few were spotted, pale as ghosts and vanishing like the same. And the rest... Well, if their bodies were ever discovered, it was only with every drop of blood drained from their corpses."

My breath caught.

He leaned closer, watching me across the flames. "You understand what I'm saying, Princess?"

I wrapped my arms around myself. Of course I did. What's more, I could see signs of it throughout my life. My stepmother refused to go out during the day. She'd spun me lies about the sunlight's damage to our skin, claiming even *I* needed to stay indoors, but the result was the same. Moreover, her servants never seemed to stay around long, leaving for reasons unknown, though others whispered ghostly tales about seeing a few of them lingering in hallways, vanishing into the shadows when spotted. And then there was the strange power she seemed to exert over everyone, making them do what she wanted.

Like believe I killed my father.

My heart ached for my servant, Fironia. I remembered her face in the moment after my stepmother whispered to her over my father's body. Was that the moment Melisandre stole her will? Had she forced Fironia to throw herself from the tower too?

Sickness twisted my stomach. Most likely.

"What does she want?" I asked quietly.

"Power," Byron said. "That's all her dark coven sought."

I looked up at him. "So are the others still out there? These... vampire witches?"

His mouth tightened. "Possibly. After the Witch War, they vanished, and no one knows why. But in all the years since, none have made a move so bold as your stepmother. Claiming a throne. Launching a veritable genocide. But it would be wise to assume they *are* out there until we can prove otherwise." He shook his head. "All of them will be hungry for power, just as their masters are."

I shivered. "So, my kingdom, then. That sort of power."

"That and more. To control a nation is to dictate the fate of thousands upon thousands of souls. To make war, if you choose, and claim even more territory under you. But beyond even that, there are the magical implications to consider. Ordinary humans gravitate toward magical power, same as giants and witches. They build cities and monuments on the very places where these power centers reside."

I swallowed dryly. "And Aneira is one of them?"

He nodded. "My only question would be why your stepmother waited so long to claim the throne for herself."

The sickened twist in my stomach grew worse. She could have killed my father at any time. Me too, for that matter. But... "Maybe she just wanted me to be old enough to blame."

Byron was quiet for a moment. "Indeed."

"But now the queen is trying to kill her," Niko pointed out, nodding toward me. "Why?"

Byron's lips thinned. "Perhaps to prevent her from trying to claim the throne. Perhaps because the magic the princess inherited from her mother is a threat." He splayed his hands. "Perhaps both... or something else entirely."

I shook my head. "But I don't have any magic." At Byron's skeptical look, I pressed on. "You've seen what it's been like these past weeks. I know what you thought, but clearly, I didn't inherit any—"

"You persist in claiming that, Princess, but I find it unlikely, given your survival on the mountainside before you found your way to our home. Clothed as you were, you should have been dead in minutes, not merely suffering minor frostbite."

I shifted position uncomfortably on the stone floor. "I can't manage even a simple spell."

"*Yet*," he countered quietly. "But the queen obviously thinks your life presents a danger to her plans, given how she's persisted in hunting you. How she's even trapped nature itself into helping her try to strike you down." He shook his head, his copper curls glinting in the firelight. "That isn't how someone behaves if they don't think you're a threat to them."

I stared at him, feeling at a loss. I couldn't believe my stepmother saw me as *dangerous*. I'd never been anything but a silly girl to her.

But what she was doing...

I wrapped my arms around myself and dropped my gaze to the flames, my body trembling. "Then you all should leave."

Silence met my words. I looked up to find them staring at me.

Dex shook his head. "We're not going to abandon you out here, Princess. And the queen will come after us no matter—"

"I know what you all said," I interrupted. "But she's after me. That tree? Whatever magic was there? It wasn't meant to hurt you. It was supposed to kill me." I shivered. "I don't want you all caught by it just because you stayed at my side."

The resistance in their eyes made my chest ache.

"Please," I begged. "I... I can't lose you all, okay? I know we've only known each other a few weeks, and please believe me when I say you've all been wonderful, but the thought she would hurt you..." I couldn't find words for it, and I shook my head instead. "Just give me a pack, and I'll—"

"All due respect, Princess," Clay cut in. "But that's not fucking happening."

"I'm nothing but a liability to you at this point."

"The hell you are," Lars replied, his voice hard.

My eyes flicked over to him, shocked to hear that tone from him.

He drew a breath, shifting uncomfortably on the ground like he'd even taken himself aback. "You're not a liability," he continued in a kinder voice. "You're our..." He stopped whatever he'd been about to say. "You matter to me. Us." His head gave a tight nod to Clay, including his brother in the statement.

Clay nodded. The others did too.

Anguish pushed at me. "You all matter to me too. That's the whole point. I can't let her hurt you because of me."

The men shared a glance with one another, some unspoken communication passing between them. And after a moment, Dex nodded, though I couldn't tell why.

"In your studies, did you ever hear the word treluria?" he asked quietly.

My brow twitched down. I shook my head.

"It's a... concept. One I didn't really believe in, at least until now."

"It means true love," Clay explained.

"Loosely translated," Byron amended.

Dex ignored them, his eyes trained on me. "It's the idea that there's someone you were made for, and who was made for you too. Stories say finding your treluria is rare, but when it happens, you know it." His mouth tightened. "I'm not saying this to pressure you, nor am I asking you to believe it too. And I'm not trying to scare you. I know there's more to... to *relationships* than some... fairytale. If a relationship is even something you want." He paused as if steadying himself. "But I feel like that's what you are to me."

Quivers spread through me. He felt that?

"Same here," Clay said.

Lars nodded, and nearby, Niko did the same, fervently.

Shocked, I glanced to Byron. He was silent, his face closed off, and I quickly dropped my gaze from his. For even a few of them to feel this about me was unbelievable, and I shouldn't expect—

"It feels that way to me as well," Byron admitted softly.

My eyes flashed back to him. He watched me, a quiet intensity to his green eyes, as if acknowledging this was as monumental as leaping from a high cliff and learning to fly on the way down.

Dex leaned toward me, drawing my focus back to him. "So there's no way in hell we're leaving you on a mountainside."

The other men made sounds of agreement.

I trembled, my eyes darting across them. Only Roan and Ozias weren't here, and maybe that was fate. They'd given no sign at all of feeling this way toward me. But from Niko's sweet smile to Clay's wry grin, Lars' encouraging look, Byron's intense gaze, and Dex's solemn one, all the men were giving me nothing but hope as they waited for what I'd say.

My insides quivered at the truth. Treluria. I'd never known the word, but when I was around them...

I wetted my lips. "I feel like maybe... you're that for me too. All of you."

Smiles broadened. Tension faded. Clay wrapped an arm around me, beaming, while Lars, Dex, and Niko just looked relieved. Byron dropped his attention to his folded hands, and I couldn't begin to guess what he was thinking from the way he'd inexplicably closed in on himself. I'd never seen him wear the oddly guarded look now on his face.

"Well, in *that* case," Clay started, grinning at me as his hand strayed down toward my breast. "What do you say—"

Gravel scraped at the entrance and I looked over sharply.

Roan stood at the cave opening.

His eerie black eyes darted over the others, pausing at Clay's hand on my chest and at something he must have seen on my face. His cold expression sank into a glower, and with careful motions, he set down the branches of firewood in his arms. "Should I come back later?"

The words were as neutral as a gray fog, and I felt my cheeks grow hot. He knew what Dex and I had done my first night at the cabin. Surely he knew of my time with Clay and Lars too. But somehow, this moment still felt awkward, and in spite of myself, I shifted a bit beneath Clay's hand as if to extract myself from the situation.

"It's fine," Dex replied evenly. "The princess just survived an attack meant to kill her, and we've all had a long day. Best choice now would be to rest, yes?" He gave Clay a pointed look, and the guy held up his hands in a gesture of surrender.

Without another word, Roan took up a piece of firewood, tossed it into the blaze, and then stalked deeper into the cave, never looking at me once.

I rolled my shoulders uncomfortably, not sure what to think.

Around me, the others rose, and several went to gather

the blankets out of their packs. Ozias returned, a string with dead rabbits hanging from his belt. He handed them to Lars before sitting by the cave opening as if intending to remain there until the mountains wore down to flat ground.

I stayed seated where I was.

"Princess," Dex said, pausing beside me. "You really should get some sleep."

I nodded, but I couldn't bring myself to get up. "What's the plan? After we sleep, I mean. If we're sticking together..." I looked up at him. "How do we all stay safe?"

For a moment, he was silent, and then he sighed, sinking down beside me. "Inherited magic or not, the queen is still trying to kill you, so we need to get you as far from her as possible. Heading deeper into the mountains isn't wise—the place is a death trap—but the nation of Gentresqua has some remote regions that could be options. The only reason we didn't head for them years ago is that our people are here. If we were ever going to stand a chance of freeing them, we needed to be close by. But if it means we're putting your life at stake if we stay..."

I looked away, guilt gnawing at me. First their home, now they had to abandon their people. They'd never asked for any of this, and yet they all were volunteering to help, even when it kept costing them.

Their nobility shamed my own because what was I doing? Running? Hiding? Letting her claim more and more of my home? And if their stories were to be believed, it wasn't a question of simply fleeing a false accusation of murder. No, I was leaving my people—and theirs—to a despotic nightmare who drank blood, stole people's free will, and would eventually try to claim the world—or at least as much as she could get her hands on while leaving the rest to burn.

My heart ached. I could never risk them, but as long as she was out there, would the risk ever truly be gone?

"How do you kill a vampire?" I asked quietly.

The cave went silent. I looked up to find the men staring at me.

"Princess," Clay started, his arms full of blankets. "You can't seriously—"

"She commands an *army*," Lars interrupted his brother, his blue eyes wide with shock.

"If I leave her to claim my country, she'll destroy the rest of the world and your people too, and then she'll come for us anyway."

The men were silent.

"I'm not talking about going up against her army. Not if I don't have to. But if there's a way to stop this, I want to take it. For my parents and for all our sakes."

The others looked at Byron, and his guarded expression fractured back into his familiar thoughtful one. "Well..." He cleared his throat, his bright green gaze dropping away to study the ground like it was one of his books. "There's the obvious: sunlight. But getting her near that would be challenging at best, as it would require breaking into the castle and all manner of difficulties. Yet"—a frown twisted his freckled face for a moment—"in the end, magic was what did this. It gave the queen her power and changed her into a vampire. If we found something tied to that, some mechanism through which to connect with her and the spell... we might be able to undermine her hold on this life. Maybe even turn those dark forces back on her." He raised an eyebrow at me. "You were around her for years. Perhaps—"

I shook my head immediately. "She never let me anywhere near her magic. She claimed it would drive me mad to see her spellwork."

Byron's frown returned.

"What about the place she and her fellow vampire witches destroyed?" Niko asked.

Everyone turned to him and the shy guy blinked, looking uncomfortable at the attention.

"What about it?" Dex asked.

Niko shrugged. "Well, she used a bunch of magic there, didn't she? Or they all did, anyway. Maybe we could pick up traces of her power? Enough to do something about it?"

"Uh, right." Clay chuckled wryly. "That means heading deeper into the mountains. Death trap, remember?"

Niko opened his mouth to argue.

"It's too risky," Roan called flatly from the shadows in the back of the cave.

Ozias made a low rumbling noise. "So is doing nothing to stop a predator who is hunting you."

Roan turned away, and even in the shadows I could see him scowling.

Ignoring him, Ozias' searing gaze slid to me and my mouth went dry. I wondered how many creatures had thought they could hide from him, only to learn they'd been horribly wrong.

"What are the odds this would help us, Byron?" Dex pressed.

The scholarly man bobbed his head thoughtfully. "It might. With the princess accompanying us, we may stand an even better chance."

I blinked, my attention snapping back to him. "Why?"

"Your mother was there. Her magic may recognize you. Offset some of the threat from the rest of the destruction."

I fidgeted awkwardly.

"Are you willing to try, Princess?" Dex asked.

Seven sets of eyes turned to me, and what could I say? No, when this could mean everything for them, for me, for both our peoples?

My head moved in a nod. "Let's do it."

24

GWYNEIRA

For a few hours, we slept, the simple need for rest finally winning out over any desire to keep moving. Dex, Clay, and Lars stayed close, holding me while Byron remained near to the entrance. A line of ore lay between him and the opening, and his hand stayed upon it as if to charge it even while he rested. But sleep couldn't claim us for long, I knew. Not if we wanted to stay as safe as possible.

Vampires were confined by sunlight. Therefore, traveling during the day meant more time to put distance between us and my stepmother.

Blinking tiredly, I forced myself to get up again as we headed out into the midday glare. On the snowy mountainside, the sun felt blindingly bright, as if by virtue of being at a higher elevation, it could bear down on us even more. The cave soon fell behind us as we climbed, and the white snow became our only surrounding. The peaks of the mountain were still high above us, and what trail the men followed, I could only guess.

"Giants have a good sense of direction," Dex told me when I asked him.

"Though somehow they often only end up with their heads up their asses," Clay chimed in.

Several of the men chuckled like it was an old joke, though of course neither Ozias nor Roan cracked a smile.

I studied the two men as we continued on. Ozias had barely even looked at me since we left the cave. The same went for Roan. Niko and Lars were hovering close, while Clay, Byron, and Dex kept an eye on me between surveying the terrain for threats even though it was daylight. But those two...

I didn't know what to make of their silence or the way they looked anywhere but me. It probably shouldn't have bothered me as much as it did. They owed me nothing, least of all connection or attraction or whatever it was I felt for them. If anything, what I had now with the others was a minor miracle. The suffering in my life had caused so much of theirs, whether through my mother's death or my father's or the false accusations leveled against me. That five of the seven of them even *spoke* to me was monumental.

But the silence still left me feeling strangely bereft.

My gaze slipped to the others. What would happen when we reached this place, if in fact we were successful and stopped my stepmother? Would these seven return to their people? Would I return to my own?

Quivers tangled in my insides. *Treluria.* The word was alien to me but beautiful. And the idea behind it...

I wanted that. Wanted *them.* I prayed there was truth to such a thing as treluria, because gods help me, I didn't want to walk away from this strange need for each of them that filled me. I'd never felt this way around anyone, and to go back to my life without them...

Some deep part of me rebelled at the thought. There *was* something between us all. Something I craved, whether its name was treluria or not. That lust filled me for them was a given, but the connection between us felt like more than that. Like I'd been waiting for them, even if I'd never known they existed, and now I dreaded leaving any of them—even Ozias or Roan, who barely looked at me.

I shook my head at myself. For a person of royal blood, that last part felt rather pathetic.

It felt rather pathetic *regardless* of blood.

The others turned, the invisible path they followed taking them down the slope again, and in silence, I continued on with them. The tree line awaited ahead, a shriveled mass of gray and green that promised some semblance of shade from the searing sun. Already, my eyes felt blinded, and whatever skin was exposed seemed to burn more from the endless light than any bitter cold. In truth, I barely felt chilled. Perhaps the winter gear Clay had conjured for me possessed even more magic than I'd assumed.

But I'd be grateful for the shelter away from the sun.

At long last, we veered past the trees and began a descent between stunted pines gnarled and twisted by decades in the savage wind. The men adjusted their arrangement around me without a word, all of them staying between me and the trees as best they could, as if to prevent any repetition of last night's attack.

I appreciated it, for while I felt I could breathe easier with some measure of protection from the wind and sun, every branch and shrub seemed ominous now.

Was my stepmother searching this far into the moun-tain range? Could she see us somehow?

Squinting, I scanned the sky. Was that eagle a servant of hers? She'd commanded countless innocent bats to their deaths, after all. Could that be another one of her thralls?

I shifted my shoulders, wishing the trees provided us more of a hiding place—and that I could trust they wouldn't try to kill me too. But the paltry excuse for a forest only grew more gnarled and skeletal the farther we walked, and by the time twilight cast the mountains in purple shadows, I felt like a bundle of nerves, throbbing with raw anxiety from every crack of a branch or call of a bird.

"Cave in half a mile," Ozias grunted from his position in the lead.

The others nodded. I glanced around, curious suddenly at his knowledge of the mountainside. I'd seen him through the windows of the cabin from time to time, slipping away from the manor and striding off by himself into the woods. But we were miles from the cabin now.

"How do you know these slopes so well?" I asked.

Ozias tensed, but he didn't turn to look at me.

"Oh, we all have our gifts, Princess," Clay explained. "Oz's are tied to the earth."

"Makes for a good miner," Lars added.

I blinked, uncertain what to say. Ozias could feel the differences in the earth enough to tell him where to find ore and caves and such, even while simply striding along?

As if sensing my confusion—or maybe out of irritation that we were discussing him at all—Ozias made a gruff noise and walked faster. Clay's lip twitched with amuse-ment, but no one said anything else as they continued on.

I followed, and as promised, in another half a mile, a

cave appeared on the mountainside as if Ozias had personally summoned it into being. Trees clustered in close around
the entrance, sheltering it from the worst of the wind, and
snowdrifts ended several feet shy of the opening, as if a
peculiar twist of the landscape had conspired to make the
fluff naturally clear itself away. The light of day was almost
entirely gone, letting stars dot the sky and turning the cave
into a black space hopefully occupied by nothing but
shadows.

We ventured inside, finding a space large enough for all
of us and thankfully dry. In short order, the men set to
arranging blankets around an open space in the center of
the cave while Lars began making a fire from the sticks and
branches he'd gathered while we walked. In only a moment,
flames began licking at the wood, spreading quickly into a
cheery blaze that beat back the cold and made all the men
appear to breathe easier.

I sank down beside the fire, removing my gloves and
then extending my hands toward the heat. My fingers felt
numb, frozen, nearly as white as the snow outside the cave
entrance itself, and despite the dancing blaze before me, I
could barely feel the warmth.

Trepidation flickered through me. Had I suffered frostbite while walking? It would make sense given how cold and
blustery it was out there, but when I tried to bend them, my
fingers moved without the slightest hesitation or resistance.
Besides the numbness, I felt fine. Not short of breath nor any
more tired than would be expected after a day of trudging
through the snow. If anything, now that I was away from
the blinding sun and the tiring trek across the mountains, I
felt better than I had all day.

I didn't remember being *this* fit, so much that a hike like that wouldn't even wind me. But perhaps Dex's training and all my activities since living at the castle had given me more endurance than I realized.

My eyes flicked up to the men around the fire, a blush touching my cheeks. There was certainly *some* exercise I hadn't yet explored today.

A tangled feeling rose in my gut as I watched them, though, and faintly, my stomach growled. I dropped my gaze away, embarrassed. Hunger should probably be attended to first, before *other* kinds of hunger could be addressed.

The twist in my gut turned to a gnawing sensation. Gods, I was famished.

Lars withdrew a bundle wrapped in a cloth from his bag. Untying the string from around the contents, he pulled the coverings aside to reveal a collection of breads and cheeses.

My stomach lurched with sudden nausea at the sight. Pressing a hand to my lips, I struggled to keep the reaction down.

He began slicing the bread and cheese with a knife from his belt.

"Where would you like to sleep, Princess?" Dex asked me.

Breathing carefully, I tried to clear the nauseated expression from my face before I looked up at him and shrugged.

He smiled. "In that case, how about you come with me?"

A thrill went through me at the commanding look in his eyes, but the feeling was distant. Hunger coupled with nausea still churned in me, making it hard to think. I could smell the bread and cheese only a few feet away, the scent bizarrely repulsive, though I couldn't understand why.

Gods, was I pregnant?

Alarm shot through my veins. Sure, I'd only slept with Lars and Clay a short while ago, but that still left Dex to consider. It'd been weeks since he'd done those delicious things to me the first night I arrived at the cabin.

I trembled, uncertain how to feel at the prospect of carrying a babe inside me. But surely it'd require more than a few weeks for the side effects of morning sickness to take hold.

Right?

My stomach wouldn't stop churning, and I couldn't lift my hand to take Dex's own. How could none of the others be revolted by what Lars was doing? How awful it smelled? What was wrong with them?

"Princess?" Concern touched Dex's voice.

My fingers dug into the gritty cave floor. I wouldn't be sick here. I just needed to move away from—

Lars made a choked noise, and my eyes snapped to him. He'd nicked his knuckle with the blade. Blood welled in the cut.

A quake rolled through my body, hunger surging again to overtake any nausea, so powerful it nearly claimed control of my muscles as well. I couldn't take my eyes from the red droplet and a desperate feeling rose in me, but I couldn't understand the reason. So he'd accidentally cut himself. Why in the world was I responding like *this*?

"Are you okay?" Byron asked, returning from the entrance where he'd been arranging a row of stones across the opening.

I couldn't respond.

"Princess?" Clay's normally joking voice was full of apprehension, but the sound came from far away. All I could see was the droplet on Lars' finger.

I lunged over to him, grabbing his wrist and licking the blood away before I could stop myself. Relief and ecstasy flooded me like I'd taken a bite of the most delicious dish in the world.

Lars yanked his hand away, shock on his face. Utter silence hung in the air as I tensed, desperate to leap after him for more.

Reality sank in on me, and a tiny breath fled my lungs as horror rolled through me in a wave of ice. Why had I done that?

My eyes crept over to the men, finding them staring at me in the firelight. No one even seemed to breathe.

"What was that, Gwyneira?" Dex asked carefully, and I shivered at the way he said my name. Like maybe I wasn't me. Like maybe I was a wild animal instead.

And he might be right. I trembled all over with the sudden craving for more of the precious blood I'd licked from Lars' finger. And that was madness. Utter, *utter* insanity.

My mouth ached, as if my teeth were begging me to bite down on someone. Anyone.

One of the men.

A whimper left me.

"Talk to us," Dex urged carefully, stepping around me to block my view of Lars. "What's happening?"

My head shook. I couldn't open my mouth for fear I'd lunge up and attack him. A drumming was starting up in my ears, discordant and arrhythmic, like my heartbeat but chaotic and coming from all around.

Gods, I wanted to go toward it. To pick one of the pounding rhythms and chase it to the ground like a wolf. I was hungry, so gods-be-damned hungry, and somehow I knew that if I could just take one of those thudding patterns down I'd be satisfied.

"Princess..." Alarm filled Byron's voice. He extracted a handful of ore from his pocket as if he was drawing a weapon but was concerned I'd attack if he moved too quickly.

I whimpered again. My teeth hurt. My body wanted to do exactly what he was afraid of and leap at him, and that terrified me.

I couldn't hurt them. I wouldn't let myself, but I wasn't safe here.

They weren't safe with me here.

Clay's hand came to rest on my shoulder, and a sudden surge of hunger nearly blinded me. My teeth bared at him, my muscles bunching to lunge upward at him.

He recoiled, his blue eyes wide.

I turned to the others, seeing the same expressions on their faces as was on Clay's. Horror. Sheer waves of it on every face. The sight cut through my hunger just enough for my muscles to be my own again.

But I could feel the ravenous drive to attack returning fast.

Crying out in desperation, I shoved away from the rocky floor and raced from the cave.

25
DEX

"Princess!" Niko cried.

Ozias caught him as he started after her. Niko stared at the cave opening, horror on his face, and the others' expressions were much the same.

Because Gwyneira had *fangs*.

I headed for the exit and Byron snagged my arm. "Don't," he warned.

"What the hell was that?" I demanded.

"I'm not sure."

"What did it *look* like?" Roan snarled. His voice thickened like he was fighting back a wave of emotion. "The queen got to her."

"What can be done?" I asked Byron, gritting out the words.

He shook his head. "Roan's right. Somehow, the queen must have infected her. Perhaps the branches..." His brow twitched down like he couldn't wrap his head around what he'd started to say.

"What?" Clay scoffed. "Had the queen's *blood* in them?"

Lars made an incredulous sound. "Twisting the natural world into poison is one thing. But this..."

"We have to go after her," Roan insisted when Lars trailed off. He strode toward the cave opening. "We'll bring her back."

"She could kill us," Byron countered.

Roan whirled at him, his black void eyes flashing with incredulity as if Byron was mad. "And if the queen reaches her first?" He turned the disbelieving expression on all of us. "No, we are *not* giving up on her, do you hear me? Whatever's happening, we will not lose her too!"

Without another word, he took off into the snow.

"Roan!" Clay yelled.

The man didn't stop.

"Dammit." Clay started after him.

I looked at the others. They all appeared shaken.

And why wouldn't they be? Our princess was in danger, and against something that I—and probably all of us—didn't have a clue how to fight. A possessed tree attacking her was one thing. But this?

A breath left me. "No one is abandoning her," I said to the rest of them. "Lars, stay here in case she circles back. Niko"—I gestured shortly to the trees around the entrance —"we need thicker cover in case the queen's minions are searching this far for her. Byron, Ozias, with me."

The others scattered quickly to do as I ordered. Bending fast, I drew a knife from my pack. Hesitating a heartbeat, I swore under my breath and then grabbed a coil of rope too.

Gwyneira had looked half feral, and whatever the queen had done to her, she may not be in her right mind. If her safety meant tying her up, I'd apologize later.

Because making sure there *was* a later for us was all that mattered.

26

GWYNEIRA

I wasn't cold. I just couldn't feel a thing.

Except hunger.

And horror.

I ran through the snow, the tears in my eyes blurring trees lit by the first rays of moonlight. Sobs racked me, turning the gnawing in my gut into agony. What was happening to me? How could I ever want to hurt Lars or the rest?

My feet moved faster. I had to get away from them, as far as I could. The idea of leaving hurt like all the fires of hell, but I couldn't risk them. Not now. Not ever. Whatever this was, I had to protect them or else I'd never forgive—

A branch caught my foot and sent me crashing to the ground, my body skidding through the snow and across the rough terrain beneath it. Shaking all over, I pushed away from the drift in which I'd finally landed, my entire being aching even worse than before.

Gods, I could barely think from the hunger.

Blinking hard, I struggled to focus past the blur of frozen

tears and pain. I was lower on the mountainside now. The trees weren't the gnarled evergreens of higher elevations. Bare branches extended all around me, the trunks gray and spreading out against the starry night sky like the finger bones of the dead clawing at the air. There wasn't a sound to be heard. Even the whisper of snow had gone silent.

But that wasn't what froze me.

From the bare branches all around, red apples dangled over the crisp white snow, bright as ornaments. A glistening substance covered them like candy syrup, making them shine in the moonlight, and at the sight my body ached even more.

Trembling, I rose to my feet, pacing toward the hanging fruit as if drawn by a tether. Whispers rose around me, fading in and out at the edge of hearing, their words unintelligible. But I didn't care. All I could see was the apple closest to me, dangling just above head height, its bright-red skin promising a sweetness beyond anything I'd ever tasted in my life.

My teeth ached. I barely noticed. Reaching up, I wrapped my fingers around the fruit. The red syrup coated my fingertips.

Calm settled over me. This would make everything better.

With a tiny jerk, I plucked the apple from the tree. The whispers became like a soothing blanket around me. I'd be okay now. This was all I needed.

I lifted the apple to my lips and my eyes drifted closed as the delicious coating slipped against the tip of my tongue. Sweet as sugar, but savory like the most nourishing meal I'd ever tasted. A smile drifted over my face as I bit down.

The heavenly flavor filled my mouth and I swallowed

quickly. I'd keep the men safe. All I needed was this delicious fruit to—

My throat convulsed.

The apple fell from my grasp as I tried to cough, but nothing came out. My hand clutched at my neck as if I could dislodge the piece of apple choking me, but I couldn't even breathe. I drove my other fist into my middle, trying to propel the fruit from my throat to no avail.

Panic thundered through me even as the world swirled, darkness gathering like a swift-moving storm. Something soft then hard hit me. The ground. My hands fumbled at my neck, at the forest floor, at anything if only it would save me, finding nothing but snow.

Voices clamored in the distance. The men crying out my name. But the whispers grew louder around me, drowning out their shouts.

And the whispers were laughter. My stepmother's laughter, ringing through my mind with victorious glee and chasing me as I fell down into the infinite dark.

27
ROAN

The monster within me would burn the world if I lost control, but right now, I wasn't sure I cared. Not with Gwyneira in danger.

I forged through the snow, my heart racing as the monstrous thing thrashed in my mind, fighting the chains I'd wrapped around it long ago. I'd only heard stories of vampires, of what they could do. But I remembered flight being part of it, and it terrified me.

Because, gods, what if she could do that? What if we'd lost her already, and she was on her way to the queen?

The creature thrashed harder.

"Princess!" I shouted, my voice tight from the strain of fighting the demon inside me. "Gwyneira, please! Don't do this!"

"Dammit, Roan, wait up!" Clay yelled behind me.

I didn't slow. I *wouldn't*. I'd nearly watched her die only hours before, and that had been bad enough. But this?

"Gwyneira!" I called again, my voice thickening as the creature tried to break free. My vision started to change, the

night glinting with red and orange light like the forest was traced by burning embers.

"Gods be damned, Roan," Clay huffed as he caught up to me. "What are you thinking, rushing off after—"

He cut off, and for a moment I feared he'd seen what I was becoming, but when I turned he was staring at something to my left. Blinking hard to shift my eyes back to normal, I followed his gaze.

The moon shone down upon a forest unlike anything I'd ever seen.

Horror rolled through me in a cold wave, inexorable. Beneath the shimmering glow of moonlight, the white snow was an eerie silver and blue, casting back enough light to reveal corruption that made the hairs on the back of my neck stand on end. Shadows twisted up the trunks of the gnarled trees like smoke, each one moving like it was alive. Coiling along the branches, the darkness was slowly retreating like a snake pulling back into its lair, but even as it went, it pulsed and twitched as if blood pumped within each tendril.

"What the *hell*?" Clay murmured beside me.

My eyes tracked along the branches. At the end of each one where a tendril of smoke tangled, there hung a rotting mass slowly crumbling away.

Red skin and molding flesh. A sickening sweetness that made my gorge rise.

Apples.

A low growl came from behind my back, startling me, and I scrambled inside to keep the creature from breaking free to retaliate against the threat. When I looked back, the others were here, but their eyes were locked on the cursed forest same as mine had been.

Except Ozias.

Still growling low, he stepped past me, his axe in one hand and his sword in the other.

My eyes tracked him, wary. I'd wondered from time to time if there was something different about him. He wasn't like me, that I knew. The demon inside me would have picked up on that. But in moments like these, I wondered if there was more to him than merely a man left in the woods when he was a child.

Rolling his neck with a crack of bones, Ozias glared at the trees. "They hid her." He sounded like it would be the last thing the forest would ever do.

"Find her," Dex ordered the others, watching the decaying fruit plunk to the earth like globs of mud. "Touch nothing."

Without a word, Ozias strode forward. Tendrils of darkness moved toward him, only to hiss with steam and smoke when he struck them with his sword and axe.

Drawing my own knife, I followed. The living shadows retreated when we sliced at them with our ore-lined blades, while all around us rotten apples hit the ground like an irregular heartbeat.

"Oh, gods." Clay's voice came from beyond the trees.

No.

Cold horror raced through me and I lunged forward, weaving fast around the gnarled trunks and leaping over misty vines. Clay was on his knees up ahead, and the dark shape in the snow before him made my heart stop.

It was the nightmare. The creature's nightmare made manifest before me.

Gwyneira lay in the snow. Her eyes were open and

unseeing, and she had one hand clasped to her throat. Ash smeared her lips and cheeks, centered around her mouth.

Clay looked up at me, horror painted across his face. "She's not breathing."

My whole body shuddered, my control cracking.

"She ate that?" Niko's incredulous voice snapped my attention around. He pointed at something on the ground only a short distance away.

An apple, black and putrid, with smoke rising from it. Even though most of it had decayed, I could still see the bite mark on its side.

Oh, gods.

"Move!" Byron shoved past me, oblivious to my battle for control, and dropped to his knees next to her. "Turn her to the side!"

Clay blinked in confusion.

"Now, dammit!"

As Clay rolled her on her side, Byron slid his arms around her, hefting her body around. With short jerking motions, he yanked his fists back, driving them into her middle over and over.

"What the hell are you doing, man?" Clay protested.

"Shut it!" He yanked his fists back again.

A piece of rotting fruit fell from Gwyneira's mouth.

Quickly, Byron shifted her around and lay her back on the snow. Holding one hand over her chest, he fumbled through his pack with his other, searching blindly and then taking out a vial. As he spoke incantations rapidly, he popped the cork from the container with his thumb and then poured the liquid into her mouth.

"Come on, baby..." Clay urged.

I couldn't even breathe, watching her.

Nothing changed.

"Dammit." Byron let the empty vial fall to the snow, shifting around. With one hand atop the other, he began compressing her chest with firm, determined motions. Her body rocked with the force of his efforts.

But still, she didn't breathe.

The demon inside me retreated as cold horror too terrible to contemplate settled over us both. "Please, no," I whispered to her. This was like before. Like always. All it took was a moment, and everything good died.

Byron pressed harder on her chest. "Dammit, please! Breathe!"

"She won't."

I whirled, knife in hand.

A woman stood several yards away, no footprints in the snow behind her and a stillness around her, as if she'd simply appeared from the landscape. Moonlight shimmered in silver over her dark skin and glowed from her fur-lined white cloak. A glistening pale green gemstone the size of a robin's egg hung from a silver chain at her neck, and an aura of power radiated from her like the depths of a still lake, tranquil now but which could contain anything.

And all around, the toxic smoke from the trees recoiled at her presence.

"The queen has killed her. Nothing you do will change that."

Ozias snarled and his hands clenched around his axe as he took a step toward the woman.

She regarded him, unfazed. "If you wish to save her, you must come with me."

"Save her?" Clay sputtered. "You just said—"

"Yes, but it's what comes next that will truly determine

her fate." Her eyes swept over all of us. "I sense love in you. What will you do for this girl?"

"Anything." The answer came from me, but the others echoed it immediately.

The woman smiled. "Good. She'll need that."

28

MELISANDRE

It was done.

Exhilaration poured through me as I felt my connection to the princess blossom from a mere potentiality into a leash. Her life extinguished like a blown-out candle, and my hold on her carried the good news of its success back to me like whispers of the damned on the air.

Nineteen years. Endless planning. And at last, the moment was here.

She was mine.

At the edge of a pond, I descended and shifted back to human form. A swipe of my hand above the still surface turned it to another kind of reflection entirely. Beneath the silvery sheen, the beings of the empty realm swirled into view, twisting like eels in a frenzy. The Voidborn could feel her potential now fulfilled, and it excited them like starved wolves on their way to a feast.

"Not long now," I whispered to them.

Their anticipation rolled over me like a wave in the air. Already, I could feel their power strengthening in me.

They'd held back—because of course they had. But now, with a witch-turned-vampire to devour, their hunger would be slaked, my pact with them would be satisfied, and unfettered power would at last be mine.

To rule the nation of Aneira would be nothing. I'd take the world. Even the others who'd joined me that fateful night, the witches of my own dark coven, wouldn't have power to compare to mine.

I chuckled to myself as I lifted into the air, flying across the mountain range toward her. Crisp moonlight shone down on the white slopes and danced across the sheer cliffs of stone. She was out there, sleeping in death, and soon, hunger would wake her. Terrible hunger that would send her ripping into everyone who'd thought to hide her from me.

And when they were dead, she would come. Untouched by cold, she'd cross the mountains to meet me because she had no choice. She was mine, and she'd walk like an obedient lamb to the slaughter because I commanded it.

"Come," I whispered. "Come to me." My lips curled. "And may all in your path die."

29
DEX

I held Gwyneira's limp form in my arms and tried not to die inside while I followed the strange woman through the snow. We'd left the poisoned forest behind, the smoky tendrils retreating from the woman and clearing a path for us all. None of us spoke, the heavy hush of the snow-covered mountainsides nothing compared to the grief pressing down on us.

But desperation was there too, spurring me onward.

We'd failed her. *I'd* failed her. All it had taken was a single moment, and even here, miles and miles from that gods-forsaken castle, the queen had still managed to steal Gwyneira's life away.

But this woman claimed it wasn't over.

I clambered awkwardly over a log, holding Gwyneira's body close. She had no pulse, no color in her skin, and her body hung like a rag doll in my arms.

But dammit, it wouldn't matter. Not when we reached our destination. This strange woman had insisted that, even while telling us we needed to hurry. Time was of the essence, though she refused to say why.

Or what she planned to actually do to save our princess.

My heart drummed in my chest, beating so hard I'd swear it was pounding for me and Gwyneira alike. Every plan I'd made and strategy I'd devised had crumbled to dust when I saw the princess lying dead on that forest floor, and now I was putting my faith in a stranger, clinging to her words like they came from the gods themselves. I knew it was madness, or at best ludicrous naivety, but I didn't care. Not now. Not when the alternative was losing Gwyneira, so if there was even a chance—

"Careful," the woman said, her calm voice breaking the silence for the first time in what felt like years and probably had only been an hour. I looked up to see her standing at the edge of a cliff with nothing but dark night and oblivion beyond. The bitter wind whipped around us, teasing snow away from the precipice in ghostly veils of white.

"Follow me precisely," she said, turning.

She stepped off the cliff.

My breath caught, but the woman didn't fall. Beneath her feet, the air shimmered like moonlight on frost, revealing a platform with the outlines of guardrails extending up on either side. Without hesitation, she took another step forward, and the glistening air solidified under her feet as if it had been waiting for her the entire time.

Like a bridge. But to what?

It didn't matter.

Drawing a steadying breath, I walked to the edge of the mountain. The night turned the mountain range into a black abyss, but every instinct I had told me death waited about six inches ahead of my toes. But the idea that the woman had brought us all this way only to fling us off a cliff seemed unlikely. And if this was how we found help for Gwyneira, I'd walk off a thousand damn cliffs.

So be it.

I took a step into the darkness.

The air supported my foot precisely where a bridge would be, and shimmers danced across the otherwise invisible surface. Instinct still demanded that I not let my other foot leave the mountain, but staying where we were wouldn't fix this.

My other foot joined the first.

I didn't fall.

A shaky breath left me. Fighting back the part of my brain that screamed I was standing in midair and would drop like a rock, I made myself walk after the woman. The air bridge glistened beneath me, hinting at a surface wherever my feet came to rest with no suggestion that the support extended farther. Only darkness waited ahead of my boots, as if every step were to be taken totally on faith, in desperate hope I'd chosen my direction wisely.

I glanced back. Byron and the others were cautiously following, their hands gripping a railing that shimmered with the same near-invisibility as the surface under my feet.

"Very brave, good giant," the woman said to me when I reached her. "A worthy warrior for the princess."

With an enigmatic smile, she turned back to the darkness and walked forward.

And disappeared.

I froze. The bridge beneath us didn't change, but the woman was no longer on it, and only the empty night sky remained where she'd been. There was no sign she'd fallen.

No shrieks or cries of terror in the darkness. It was as if she'd simply ceased to exist.

"Come, good giant. We haven't long."

Her voice carried around me on the frigid wind like the memory of a dream. I tightened my hold on Gwyneira. This could be a trick. Some minion of the queen's sent to torture us with a game.

But what were our options?

I walked forward.

A tingling feeling passed over my skin, like frost spreading across my body, and then suddenly the darkness before me was transformed. A sheer mountain cliff appeared ahead, topped in snow and glistening in the moonlight. White wooden staffs were planted upright along the edge, crystalline blue flames dancing on them like winter moonlight come to life. Glistening glass balls of light hung in midair beyond them, hovering unsupported over the entire top of the cliff and shining like stars were held inside.

On the ledge, the woman waited. Renewed trepidation rose in me at what I was seeing, even as instinct made me want to run for the solid ground ahead. Holding Gwyneira close, I made myself walk carefully across the shimmering bridge until at last rock and snow were beneath my feet once more.

"What is this place?" I asked, eyeing the woman and the area around us with equal wariness. Beyond the wooden staffs, a raised platform waited, circular and having no purpose I could see. The sides of the mountain continued upward beyond that, though from the way the snow drifts parted, it looked like a path extended between the slopes.

The woman smiled and glanced back over her shoulder as three figures in white robes appeared on the trail between the mountain slopes as if they'd simply materialized from the snow itself. I couldn't see their faces beneath the hoods of their fur-lined cloaks. Even their hands were invisible, tucked into their sleeves and folded before them. Chains of shining platinum hung from their necks, the one at the center bearing a ruby the size of my fist, while the one to the left wore a smaller sapphire and the one on the right carried an emerald. The power rolling off the trio of figures made me want to retreat, though only invisible bridges and certain death waited at my back.

"Welcome, dwarves."

I froze at the name only our own people knew. The warm voice held a trace of amusement, and when the figure at the center of the trio lifted their hands to lower their hood, the speaker's face held a slight smile too. Her hair was the color of tempered steel and shot through with thick swaths of pure white, while her dark eyes seemed to see everything about us in a single glance. Though fine lines showed on her olive skin, hinting at the far side of middle age, her back was rigidly unbowed. I had the impression she could strike us all dead before we even realized she had attacked, every ounce of our training in fighting and magic be damned.

"Who are you?" Clay asked her, coming up beside me. Byron stood on my opposite side, while the others flanked them. Gripping his axe, Ozias glowered as if he'd see anyone who tried to harm us sent straight to hell.

"I am Leontine, Gwyneira's godmother."

"You're the Jeweled Coven," Byron said, disbelief in his voice.

"What remains, yes. Those Gwyneira's mother was able to save. And like you, warrior dwarves, we've stayed in hiding for many years." She smiled. "Waiting for the princess."

My brow twitched down. We hadn't been waiting on anything. We'd only been trying to stay alive long enough to help our people.

"She said you could save her." Clay jerked his chin at the woman who'd led us here.

Leontine nodded. "Indeed. In truth, it is the seven of *you* who will save her—if she can be saved at all."

"What's that mean?" he demanded.

Not answering, Leontine looked out across the expanse beyond the cliff as if she'd heard something on the wind. Without turning her attention from the darkness, she gestured sharply to her two companions, who moved immediately to climb the steps to the raised platform.

"Kamaria," she said shortly.

The woman who'd led us here nodded briefly and turned to face the cliff. Lifting her hands, she began chanting in a low voice, and the hairs on the back of my neck rose to feel the magic stirring in the air.

"What's going on?" Niko asked worriedly.

"The queen is calling her. We haven't much time." Leontine looked back at us, her dark eyes seeming to peer straight into our souls. "If you wish to see Gwyneira restored to herself, we must act now." Her expression was grim. "And you must be ready for anything."

30
GWYNEIRA

Death was anything but silent.

Come to me... come to me...

The whisper permeated everything. It was my only thought. My only memory. In the darkness and the emptiness, it was the guiding star, calling me, drawing me toward it where everything would be calm and everything would make sense. I couldn't fight it, but I couldn't even remember why I would have wanted to. I'd been created for this purpose, and there had been nothing before it. Nothing after.

Only the whisper. Only the command.

Only pain.

I writhed in the darkness as agony began to gnaw at me. Like a rot that consumed everything in its path, deep hunger spread through my core and out into all I was, leaving nothing in its wake. I *was* the hunger. Only it remained, an empty hollow that demanded to be filled.

All in your path will die...

Need filled me, twisting me. I had the answer, and it

carried through my body like a wave, changing everything in its path. My mouth ached, but then the pain receded. My muscles burned, but then that agony faded too. When I opened my eyes, the world was a kaleidoscope of light in which I could pick out every shimmering detail. Glass globes hung in the sky, shining like someone had trapped the stars. Hard rock was beneath my back, and my mind knew it to be cold though my body didn't care. A drumming filled my ears, discordant and coming from all around, but delicious and calling to the emptiness I felt inside.

I needed it. Wanted it. *Craved* it.

"Gwyneira."

I sat up sharply, my eyes snapping toward the sound, even if I didn't recognize the word. Was it a name? I had none. Only obedience to the commands of the voice in my mind.

Figures surrounded me on all sides, forming a circle atop a platform of gray marble and white stone. Seven men, and as one they stepped toward me.

They each held a knife in their fists.

I snarled, surging to my feet with barely an effort, the air bending around me as if terrified to be in my path. The men thought to attack, but I could hear that delicious drumming and now I knew its source.

Kill them all...

I darted at the nearest one, a man with blond hair, summer-blue eyes, and not a chance in hell of stopping me.

His knife slashed, but not in my direction.

I stopped. Blood dripped from the slice he'd made across his wrist to splash on the stone platform, and my eyes couldn't help but drop to it. Hunger roiled my insides, overriding every other consideration.

I lunged at him, taking him from his feet as my teeth sank into his wrist around the slash. Hot blood poured into my mouth and I gulped it down greedily, craving more and more. It was what I'd needed, and it brought heat back to the world like pure fire flooding my veins.

Kill them all...

I drew deeper on the vein beneath my teeth, desperate to drain it dry, but before I could, the sound of footsteps drew my attention. I looked up to see a copper-haired man extending his wrist to me as well, a gash across his flesh.

Hunger gripped me all over again. I leapt at him, taking his wrist in my teeth and swallowing the ambrosia of blood that followed. It wasn't the same as the other. A different flavor of blessed wine, and I reveled in it.

Kill them!

I sucked down more of the delicious blood, eager to do as commanded. Nothing but the voice mattered. Nothing but the voice existed, and I had to obey. But then more footsteps sounded near me. More wrists extended like an offering, dripping red and beautiful.

I couldn't resist.

Turning from the copper-haired man, I leapt at the next, a younger one this time. His blood was like flowers and earth, filled with the warmth of springtime.

Images flashed in my mind. Pink blossoms growing like magic from a single branch. A tentative smile, so gentle and kind.

I left him and turned swiftly to the next. A pale one with eyes like the black abyss of a starless night, who tasted like a mix of burning embers and wood that wouldn't break no matter the storm.

Pitch-black eyes watching me from the shadows, their bottomless depths filled with a sadness I didn't understand.

What is this?

I pulled back at the confusion of the voice inside me. Its sound wasn't as clear as it had been. But before I could question, another wrist appeared, promising more flavors I hadn't tasted and more deliciousness I couldn't help but need. Grasping it tightly, I tugged it to my mouth.

Giants? No!

The command made me falter, but the blood was already pouring between my lips. Another blond man this time, a mirror of the first one I'd tasted. Pain and hope mixed in his eyes like the churning waves of the sea, ever mercurial and powerful. He tasted like it too, salty as the ocean I'd only seen once, long ago when I was a child.

Leave them and come!

"Come here, girl," said a bearded man as he extended his scarred wrist as well. His voice was gruff, and when I took his wrist, his blood tasted like iron and bone, and like the dark depths of the earth that no land-dwelling eyes had seen. With a firm grip, he held my head, keeping my mouth to his vein.

You will leave this place and return to me now!

I twitched, but I didn't want to go. There was one left. A dark-haired man with light brown skin whose face sent images of a knowing smile flashing through my mind, even while my body tingled as if it felt a sinfully delicious touch. I had not yet tasted him, and already, he was offering his blood to me.

Obey me!

My teeth sank into his wrist.

The earth shifting. The ground yielding anything he

needed. Growth was his power, and as his blood entered my mouth, it joined with all the others. The essence of the seven men around me mingled inside my body, spreading and bringing with them scene after scene, like lights coming on in a playwright's theater. The cabin and the clearing. The snowy mountains and the castle and—

My father. His dead body on the ground. My stepmother claiming it was me.

I command you!

I flinched back, my teeth leaving Dex's wrist as the order ricocheted through my mind. My muscles ached like the voice had sunk fishhooks into them and now tugged at me as if with string. I was to be its puppet. *Her* puppet, meant to destroy everyone.

And for what?

Return to me!

I shook my head. "No."

A hush fell inside me. All around, the men sank down at my sides, their hands resting on my shoulders and back, their gentle touch like an anchor to this place.

To them.

But the command inside me fought to overpower them. Corruption still sank its hooks into every tiny particle of my being. How long had this been a part of me? How long had this been waiting?

A bloodthirsty chuckle played through my mind.

So be it.

Darkness surged in my mind as shouts broke out all around me. I looked up in horror as figures suddenly raced closer in the night sky, resolving as if from shadow. Melisandre. Others I recognized as servants and soldiers who'd vanished years before. They slowed above the cliffside, hovering in the sky above the glistening balls of light, their skin drained of color in death.

My stepmother's lips pulled back, her fangs shining in the blue-white firelight. "You thought to hide from me, and yet you brought my thrall right to your doorstep." She smiled. "Ever the fools."

She threw her arms wide and the darkness came to life behind her. Whips of shadow lashed out at the glistening lights, shattering them and sending glass raining down on the cliffside below. Her servants dove at the gaps, darting through them and speeding toward us.

Below the platform, figures in white robes lifted their arms, and lightning crackled up at the sky, tearing into the vampires. But too many raced at them, evading the bolts, and I watched in horror as the vampires ripped one of the figures from the ground and flung them into the darkness beyond the cliff.

And still the vampires were coming.

"You're mine, Gwyneira," my stepmother called. "You have been since you first tasted my blood in your baby cradle." She extended her hand. "It only took your death to awaken your true nature."

A choking feeling gripped my body, as if an invisible tether had just tightened in every part of me. I tried to pull away, but there was nowhere to go. I was as trapped as a moth in a spider's web.

She jerked her hand upward. I was suddenly yanked away from the platform, up and up into the night sky as my giants shouted in horror behind me. My hands scrambled at my throat, but I couldn't stop myself from flying into the night, racing closer to my stepmother until I hung suspended only a few yards from her with all of oblivion open beneath me.

The darkness seethed around her, shapes just on the edge of sight, as if they slithered somehow between the moonlight and darkness. Dark ghosts of tentacles lined by thorns. Eel-like faces with razor-sharp teeth. Whispers ghosted around me, their words just beyond my ability to hear, but I bit back a scream when the sound seemed to crawl inside my mind all the same.

My stepmother's red lips drew back in a smile. "You are my sacrifice. With your death, my bargain is complete, and all the power of the empty realms will be mine." Her hands rose. "You never had a chance of stopping me."

The shadowy tentacles surged forward, sweeping past her to wrap around me. They were like mist and ether, unreal, yet their sharp thorns bit into my flesh, and I screamed as poison poured into the ghostly wounds, burning like acid. There was no escape from them. Nowhere to turn or run. The ghostly vines stabbed like knives, and past my cries, all I could hear was my stepmother's laughter.

Because she'd won.

I thrashed and twisted, unable to escape. Below me, the giants slashed at the vampires, holding them back with their weapons though the creatures surrounded them on all sides. Lightning lanced the sky from the cloaked figures below, but it scattered, useless against the shadowed tentacles teeming in the night.

Who was I against this? What could I do against a witch who'd cursed me only days after I was born?

My vision blurred with tears. The precious memories I'd reclaimed scattered like stars in my mind to be swallowed by the dark poison writhing within me, devouring my soul. The flecks of my life were so infinitesimal against the never-ending, hungry hell that she'd cast me into, nothing but dust and fragile light as white as snow.

White as snow...

The fading thought echoed through my mind, the voice so familiar and yet not my own. Comfort came with it, and a thump passed through me like a heartbeat though my heart had long since gone still, pumping something more than my own blood.

Red as blood...

The darkness was shifting. Churning. But something else was inside me now, deeper than the pain.

Dark as ebony...

I was more than blood, more than muscle and bone, fang and claw. There was something within me that had slept for longer than the years a vampire's blood had been in my veins, and now...

I send the seven to my daughter...

I opened my eyes. Energy flowed through me, vibrant with a sensation like the air before a lightning strike. The darkness flinched back, still writhing its thorn-covered tentacles. Below me, my giants fought, and love swelled inside my chest for them. I wouldn't let them down.

I turned, the thrashing tentacles tangling around me, but they couldn't come close to me anymore. In the night sky, my stepmother hovered, laughing as her minions attacked everyone below. But then she caught sight of me again.

"What?" she cried. "How?"

And you will never win.

I smiled.

Energy surged inside me, building like all the heavens would come crashing down. Spring and fire, the summer sky and the earth below. The forest and the dark caves and all that tied them together as one. Seven powers, united by what she had intended to be their destruction, and held together by the eighth.

Me.

A wave of magic exploded from me, slamming into her and the shadowy tentacles. The creatures' deafening screams ripped through the night, and all of reality seemed to shatter like a mirror at the sound. A sense of infinite distance suddenly filled the night, but through the cracks in the sky, they retreated as if fleeing this world.

One of the tentacles swept out, catching my stepmother's waist. Her eyes went wide, her face overwhelmed with absolute horror.

"No!" she shrieked. Her hands reached for me, grasping at the air. "No, Gwyneira, don't let them—"

They ripped her backward through a gash in the night sky.

And then she was gone. The cracks in the air vanished, leaving only silence, and like a wisp of smoke, the feeling of a tether around me vanished. I was free of her. Free of the creatures to which she'd tried to sacrifice me, as well.

But unlike the vampires now fleeing from the cliffside, I didn't know how to fly.

Gravity took hold of me. I screamed as I fell into the night.

31
GWYNEIRA

In my dream, I walked through corridors I'd known all my life, each twist and curve so familiar. I ran my hand along the walls, feeling the warm stones thrum beneath my fingertips. Even if it was only my imagination, I'd swear they welcomed me back again.

Because I was home.

Echoes reached my ears, carrying from a time long gone. My father's laughter. My own childhood voice telling him stories of a little bird and all it had to say. So many happy times, no matter what came later.

At the top of the spiraling hall, I came to her door. For only the second time in as long as I could remember, it hadn't been shut fully, and past the opening, light and shadow played across the walls.

But that couldn't be allowed to persist. Not here. Not anymore.

I put a hand to the wood. At my touch, it swung wide.

The room was empty, the shutters open to the black night, and everything of her spells hidden in plain view—a vial here, a jar there. They stood out to me now, as if a glow just beyond sight hovered around them. At the center of the room, a round table held a slender knife, a black ribbon, a glistening comb, and a bowl of red apples.

But beyond it all, the mirror hung, and its surface didn't reflect the room. Instead, an endless gray expanse waited there, a place where light and color came to die. In the abyss, shadowy things swam, vicious and eternally hungry. Even as I watched, their arms reached out, trying to escape the mirror, and their whispers hissed through the room.

"No." I took a step closer. "This is my castle. You're not allowed here any longer."

The whispers grew louder. *Our power is in you...*

"There's more in me than that."

Reaching down to the table at my side, I took up one of the glistening red apples and held it before my lips.

"For my mother," I whispered.

The surface of the apple turned hard as a ruby in my hand.

I flung it at the mirror.

Glass shattered, raining down onto the floor and taking oblivion with it. Only a stone wall remained behind the empty gilded frame, and from the air, the sense of infinite space drifted away as if it'd never been.

I smiled.

"Gwyneira..."

My eyes turned to the window. In the distance, the mountains waited, their snowy slopes stone gray against the night sky. I'd fallen. I remembered that now. Fallen into the night. But now Dex called to me.

"Princess, come back to us."

Byron.

"Wake up, girl."

Ozias.

"Come on, Princess. Please."

Niko.

"Hey, no time for napping."

I smiled. Clay.

"We need you to wake up now."

Lars.

Silence followed, and then a soft whisper as if he was right at my ear. "Please, not you too."

Roan, with so much pain in his voice that I turned as if to reach for him.

And the room was gone. I lay beneath a night sky, globes of light hovering above me, and something soft supported my back. Snow drifted down, dancing beneath the lights like tiny stars.

Dex sat on the ground, his arms holding me, and the others were all around us, their hands on me.

"Princess?" Byron said warily.

Relief flooded me as I stared at them. "You're alive." I reached a hand up toward them, and Clay grasped it, holding it tight in both of his own. A bandage wrapped his wrist, and each of the other men's too, though bloodstains peeked around the edges. "You're—"

I caught sight of my own flesh, and shock stilled my words.

Barely any trace of color remained.

"White as snow," I whispered.

Clay's brow twitched down with confusion.

I couldn't explain. My mouth still felt strange, and suspicion suddenly gripped me. Cautiously, I ran my tongue over my teeth, and a tiny sound of shock escaped me.

Fangs.

I trembled. My heart wasn't beating, and my breath was still, and of the winter chill around me, I couldn't feel a thing at all.

"I'm... I'm still like her."

"No," Dex said immediately. "Nothing like her."

I looked up at them. "Are you all okay?"

"Yeah," Niko said.

"Hey, I needed another scar," Clay added.

Guilt gripped me. "I'm sorry. I couldn't stop—"

His grip tightened on my hand, his humor vanishing into reassurance. "We're okay, Princess. Promise."

I hesitated and then gave a small nod. When I moved to rise, Dex helped me up, never letting go, and the others stayed close, touching me like they were trying to anchor me here.

It was comforting. Their blood pulsed through me, myriad powers braiding through my veins like threads of light. But along with it, a strange energy thrummed through my body. It felt familiar, as if it'd been there the whole time, I just hadn't realized it.

How much had her blood inside me held me back, keeping me from feeling the magic I had inside? How much more than a vampire's powers had been unleashed in me when I woke up from death?

I shuddered. I'd figure it out, but later. Now, we were alive and she was gone. And that was all that mattered.

Because there was a kingdom to claim. A people to free.

Love to explore.

I looked at the others. What wonder and miracle had brought them into my life when I thought I'd lost every-thing? I could barely speak from gratitude for it. Together, we stood upon the platform where first I'd woken, all of us safe. On my right, the mountain continued up into the night sky, while to my left, the ground ended in a cliff and darkness that swirled with ghostly snow.

A shiver ran through me. But I hadn't fallen there. Hadn't died.

I caught sight of the cloaked figures beyond the platform and I tensed. Wooden staves topped by glowing blue-white flames formed a border at the cliff's edge behind them, illuminating them with eerie light. An electric feeling of power radiated from them, like the air was more compressed and charged where they stood.

Magic. It had to be. I could feel it now, around them and the men alike, different for each but powerful all the same.

"Hello, Gwyneira," said the one at the center.

"Who are you?" I replied, my voice held steady by willpower alone.

The woman's hands rose, and gray hair streaked with white shone in the eerie light as she lowered her hood.

She smiled. "The ones who've been waiting for you."

32
MELISANDRE

The hard ground slammed into my side, and the shrieking hurricane of nothingness shredding me became a crash of waves.

On shaking limbs, I pushed myself up from the wet stone. I lay on a rocky outcropping beside a black sea. The night overhead was starless, choked by clouds, and every few moments, a spray of seawater erupted from the waves below, soaking the stone and me alike.

But I wasn't dead.

I *should* have been dead.

Feeling flayed on the inside and yet strangely heavy, I looked down the coast. In the distance, a lighthouse glowed, its fires burning bright against the night. I had to be miles from the mountains. Miles from the capital city too. I'd never seen this place before in my life.

"Hello," came a voice, hissing and sibilant.

I tensed. No.

A dark chuckle behind me made my skin crawl. Warily, I turned, looking over my shoulder.

An eel-faced man stood on the rocky outcropping, his gray skin like a glistening wet seal and his eyes nothing but black slits. He smiled at me, too many teeth inside his mouth, all of them glinting like metal and drawn down to razor-sharp points. "Thanks for the ride into your world."

Gwyneira and her men are about to face a threat unlike anything they've ever seen. Find out what happens next in **Of Blood So Red**, available now!

TITLES BY SIERRA ROWAN

The Vampire Rebellion Series

Blood Pawn

Blood Captive

Blood Rebel

Blood Queen

Forever After: Crimson Snow

Of Snow So White

Of Blood So Red

Of Fate So Dark

Of Nine So Bold

ABOUT THE AUTHOR

Sierra Rowan is the USA Today Bestselling author of action-packed reverse harem paranormal romance and urban fantasy novels. Sierra loves to write stories filled with steam, heart, and adventure where a happily-ever-after is guaranteed, even if it takes a few magical battles and wild escapes to get there.

Get updates about all of Sierra's books at sierrarowan.com.

amazon.com/author/sierrarowan

bookbub.com/authors/sierra-rowan

goodreads.com/sierrarowan

facebook.com/authorsierrarowan

x.com/SierraRowanBook

instagram.com/authorsierrarowan

tiktok.com/@sierrarowanbooks